STOLEN RIVER

RIVER

A SHAWNEE ADVENTURE

also by

BOB GIEL

A CROW TO PLUCK
SHAWNEE
SAVING THE TELL

STOLEN RIVER

A SHAWNEE ADVENTURE

BOB GIEL

HAT CREEK

HAT CREEK

an imprint of
Roan & Weatherford Publishing Associates, LLC
Bentonville, Arkansas
www.roanweatherford.com

Library of Congress Cataloging-in-Publication Data
Names: Giel, Bob, author
Title: Stolen River/Bob Giel | Shawnee #3
Description: First Edition. | Bentonville: Hat Creek, 2024.
Identifiers: LCCN: 2024941519 | 978-1-63373-969-7 (trade paperback) |
ISBN: 978-1-63373-970-3 (eBook)
Subjects: FICTION/Westerns | FICTION/Action & Adventure |
FICTION/Thrillers/Historical
LC record available at: https://lccn.loc.gov.2024941519

Hat Creek trade paperback edition June, 2024

Cover & Interior Design by Casey W. Cowan
Cover art by Frederic Remington (1861-1909)
The Winchester, Oil on canvas
Editing by George "Clay" Mitchell, Anthony Wood, Don Money & Amy Cowan

For Rachel

1

THE BLOW TO THE BACK of Jeremy Banning's head made a sharp crack as it rendered him instantly senseless and opened a bloody wound at the impact point just below the brim of his hat. Grael Renquist watched as his partner's body collapsed and pitched forward, the result of the strike he delivered. But Renquist couldn't just leave Banning's lifeless body here for anyone to find. He pitched it over the cliff watched as it fell striking the side of the mountain to the ground below.

Landing heavily on the craggy boulders that lined both sides of the creek, the unconscious victim was smashed and crushed against the immovable objects. Bones were broken. Organs were rendered inoperative. Face and forehead were shattered, causing an instant, bloody demise.

Renquist stared at the branding iron in his hand, the instrument he, seconds before, used to dispense the blow that sent Banning careening over the precipice. He moved forward to the edge to observe the result of his handiwork. Banning's twisted form lay spread-eagled on the inclined surface of jagged rocks and boulders. Blood was already coursing from the many wounds sustained in the fall, staining the rocks as it leaked downward. Renquist had no doubt he had accomplished his purpose. As he looked down, his mind backtracked over the events that ultimately led to this act.

A YEAR EARLIER, 1864, THE American Civil War ground to a halt. While this conflict engulfed much of the country, it had little direct effect on the territory of Colorado. With very few warring encounters occurring this far west, the territory was left alone to deal with its own major problem, the Cheyenne and Arapahoe population. To solve this dilemma, Colorado formed a militia headed by United States Army Colonel John Chivington, an expressed enemy of the Indians. The situation culminated that year in the infamous Sand Creek Massacre during which Chivington led a superior force against a peaceful encampment of the natives, slaughtering helpless men, women, and children indiscriminately.

Renquist, a Swedish immigrant, joined the militia to portray the image of a good citizen. He rode with the troops on that mission. However, Grael Renquist was more of an opportunist than a soldier. A ranch owner in eastern Colorado near the Front Range area, Renquist's explorations of the region turned up a creek that was fed by the runoffs of mountain snows to the west. Its route flowed south of Renquist's land but presented the possibility, if dammed and diverted, of keeping his ranch endlessly supplied with water. Renquist determined to accomplish this to ensure an unlimited supply to his land. This would lessen the supply to the surrounding ranchers, but he could turn that to his advantage by selling them what they needed. He concocted a plan to accomplish both purposes.

A day before the Sand Creek incident, Renquist slipped away from the march and headed back to the Front Range. Along the way, he picked up men and supplies sufficient to build a makeshift dam across the creek. He paid no heed to the fact that the land on which the creek emanated was populated by the Cheyenne. When the Cheyenne discovered the white man's encroachment, Renquist countered their threats by promising payment for the privilege of using the creek. The Indians agreed to Renquist's terms, basically delaying payment until he turned a profit. After the construction of the dam, the waterway was diverted and directed toward the Renquist ranch. This new stream he named Sorrel Creek, passing it off as a freak of nature that simply appeared out of nowhere.

While the massacre at Sand Creek dominated Colorado's attention, the Sorrel Creek affair went virtually unnoticed until the original channel's course dried up and caused a shortage to ranches south of Renquist's property. Like the good neighbor he purported to be, Renquist offered to supply them from his new source. His price was not questioned since the businesses would fail without water.

The plan functioned well for some time until it was determined that the dam was beginning to give way. A much more effective and substantial barrier would be required. Unable to finance that venture alone, Renquist sought assistance. To that end, in late 1865, he set out to pay a call on his neighbor to the east, Jeremy Banning.

THE BANNING SPREAD WAS CONSIDERABLY smaller than Renquist's GR holdings, thus requiring the labors of only a few hands. Banning spent his days working the ranch alongside his employees, returning home each evening exhausted.

As the sun sank behind the mountains in the distance, he rode slowly toward the main house after dismissing the hands for the evening. Drawing rein at the rail out front, he swung wearily from the saddle. The door flew open and seven-year-old Foy Banning bounded onto the porch and launched his chunky body directly at his father.

"Papa!" the boy called as he landed heavily in Banning's arms.

Banning grunted and bounded backward a step while gripping the boy. He managed to prevent both from falling. "You're going to get hurt you keep doing that, Foy," he said in a high pitched voice with a Midwestern twang. "I told you that before."

The boy was immediately contrite. "I know, Papa. I'm sorry." His voice was husky. "I'm just glad you're home."

A fairly slight man of average height, Banning lowered Foy to the ground and laid his hand on the boy's head. "Well, I'm glad to *be* home, son, but I'm not up to playing with you right now."

"You don't got to, Papa. You can just be home with us."

"I can do that. Why don't you ask Meelee to get supper going while I see to my horse."

"Yes, Papa." Foy turned and headed back up the porch steps.

Banning watched his son, noting again the differences between himself and Foy. The boy's hair was straight and a light, almost blond color and he was tall for his age. These were traits passed on not by Banning, but by his late wife. Even Foy's round face, completely different from Banning's long, bony countenance, was almost an exact duplicate of hers. Good thing. The boy would be better looking than his father, thank the Lord.

As Foy crossed the threshold, Banning turned to his horse and picked up the reins. The barn was situated a short distance to the right of the small, modest house. He ducked under the horse's neck and led the animal in that direction, walking slowly. Movement in the distance caught his eye and caused him to stop. He looked in that direction as a figure on horseback approached.

In the limited light allowed by dusk, Banning had difficulty identifying the person riding toward him. He waited the seconds it took for the visitor to come close enough and then was able to make out his neighbor, Grael Renquist.

"Good evening, Banning," Renquist said. His voice was hoarse and had a distinct Scandinavian accent. He spoke in a slow, measured tone.

Banning acknowledged him. "Evening, Renquist. What brings you out this evening?"

Their words were an indication of their relationship, that of neighbors who were casually acquainted but not deeply involved in each other's lives. Renquist continued to within a few feet of where Banning stood. He stopped and dismounted. "I have a proposition for you."

"Oh? What's on your mind?"

"I need a partner."

Banning studied the tall, gaunt man before him. Renquist had the wisp of a smile on his narrow face. This was a look Banning had never seen before. Having known Renquist for several years casually, he could not recall a time when he had seen him smile. Additionally, he was totally confused by Renquist's statement.

"Afraid I don't understand. Partner for what?"

Renquist's face changed to a grin. "You are no doubt aware that the water we share comes from Sorrel Creek. What you don't know is that the creek did not simply appear as I originally explained. I created it."

Banning's face crinkled up in a change from lack of understanding to complete confusion. He remained silent and allowed Renquist to continue.

"Yes, I created it." Renquist seemed to answer a question present in Banning's mind, but one he never asked. "I explored up in the Front Range some time ago and discovered a water source that originates from far up in the mountains. I calculated that if I dammed that stream and diverted it, I could supply my land and, by extension, your land with unlimited water. But the dam is not holding. It must be replaced by one of better construction. In order to do this, I need financial help. I cannot afford to rebuild the dam on my own."

Banning studied Renquist for a second. "You asking me for money?"

"No, I would never do that. I'm offering you a partnership. After the dam is rebuilt, we will sell the water to our neighbors. Right now, you and I are the only ones who have enough water. The others must continually conserve their water in order to have enough for essentials. Their lands are simply not situated properly to have access to anything more than the winter runoffs. They will have to continue to make do with that. We can remedy that for them, though, and, at the same time, make a small profit. All that is required is an initial investment from you to match mine. Then we can go ahead and start the construction."

"Why me?"

"Why not you? Banning, this is a once in a lifetime opportunity. Why not you? Why should you not share in this opportunity? Don't you want to be able to save some money instead of putting everything back into your business? I know I do."

Banning thought for a moment, seriously thought about Renquist's proposal. This may be the opportunity he needed to start saving for Foy's future.

"How much would you need?"

Renquist seized upon Banning's interest. "To erect an adequate structure, I would need ten thousand dollars. I have only five thousand available. Your investment would be the remaining five thousand."

Banning breathed an apprehensive sigh. "Five thousand. That'll be tough to pull together."

"I would not need it all at once. The project would be paid for in stages over the course of the construction. All I need right now is your commitment and whatever you can offer initially so we can begin."

Banning gave it more thought. Renquist waited. There was a look of confidence on Renquist's face. He did not push the situation further.

"I'm interested," Banning said after a few seconds. "But I need more information."

"Of course. I would expect no less. Why don't you come to my place in the morning? I'll tell you everything you need to know. I have maps and plans to show you. And then, if you want to proceed, we can have the partnership papers drawn up straight away."

"All right. I'll stop by after breakfast."

Renquist burst into a broad smile and shook Banning's hand vigorously. "Excellent!"

BANNING ARRIVED AT RENQUIST'S HOME later that morning. Renquist greeted him and invited him in. On the kitchen table, Renquist displayed a hand-drawn map to illustrate the location of the water source.

"Here is the position of the present dam," he said. He pointed to the spots on the map as he explained. "This is the diversion point. Unfortunately, the dam was somewhat haphazardly built and is now showing pronounced signs of collapse. It is already leaking in several places."

"How long before it lets go?" Banning asked.

"I asked that question of the engineer I engaged for the project. His answer was that there was no way of knowing for certain. He recommends the new construction be begun as quickly as possible."

Renquist unrolled a set of engineering plans for the new structure. "These are the plans for the new dam," he said. "It will be placed just forward of the existing structure. Once it is finished, the old dam will be destroyed and removed. That will prevent interruption of the diversion of the creek."

Banning studied the map and the plans at length, satisfying his every question before needing to ask it. Everything was laid out intelligently, as he would have done it himself.

"Do you have any questions?" Renquist asked.

"I can't think of any that haven't already been answered."

"Then, can I count on your participation?"

Banning nodded. "I'm in. When do you need the money?"

"If you can give me three hundred this week, I'll retain the engineer and get him started. I'll let you know when we reach the next phase."

"I'll have it for you tomorrow... partner." Banning smiled and extended his hand.

Grinning, Renquist shook the hand vigorously. "Yes, yes, partner."

Over the next few months, the engineer was contracted and a crew was hired. The new dam was begun a short distance from the old structure. Upon its completion, the faulty one was dismantled and removed. At each stage, Banning dutifully contributed his portion of the funds as they became required.

Without notoriety, the Renquist and Banning Water Company began conducting business. In low-key visits to his neighbors, Renquist announced the availability of the new water supply. He offered contracts to each of them at prices that he said were necessary to cover the cost of maintaining the dispensing equipment. With no other option available, the ranchers were forced to sign on.

Banning, busy with his own ranch duties, allowed Renquist to carry out the details of the agreements alone and unsupervised. He accepted his share of the profits without question.

As time passed, Renquist raised prices. There was some push-back, but the customers, left with no alternative, ultimately accepted the increase and Renquist's excuse that maintenance and equipment costs had increased. He pocketed these additional profits and continued to pay Banning on the basis of the original contracts. Banning accepted his share, trusting Renquist. In fact, Banning never questioned Renquist about anything regarding the venture.

―――――――

ONE NIGHT, SHORTLY AFTER THE increases took effect, Banning sat down to dinner with Foy and Foy's governess, Meelee.

Amelia Scocroft had come into the Banning home two years earlier when Banning's wife suffered a debilitating stroke. Amelia was twenty-two at the time. Slim and tall, she had vibrant features and bright, penetrating blue eyes. She possessed superior intelligence and had, from the start, taken charge of the Banning household. Young Foy had difficulty pronouncing her name, shortening it to Meelee. The name stuck.

Banning's wife never recovered from the stroke and, after several months of incapacitation and steady decline, she succumbed.

After the funeral, Banning asked Meelee to stay on to run the home and to help raise Foy. She agreed and quickly became an integral part of the Banning household.

During dinner, Banning spoke to Foy. "You now have a bank account. All the money I make from the water company is going into it. Although you can't use it now, there should be quite a decent amount there when you come of age."

Foy, was unimpressed. "Why can't I use it now?"

"Because it's for your future. You'll appreciate having it later in life."

Meelee changed the subject. "I heard something in town today that I thought you should know about."

Banning turned his attention to her as she continued. "I was in the store and two of our neighbors were there discussing the price they pay for water. They seemed to think it was excessive. When they realized I could hear them, they changed the subject and walked away."

"That's strange. We only charge what's necessary to cover expenses and to make a small profit. Why would they think it's excessive?"

"I don't know, but they seemed quite upset over it."

"Who were they?"

"Missus Adams and Missus Cane."

Banning pondered for a second. "I think maybe I should have a talk with them. I don't want any bad blood starting."

Meelee showed further concern. "I know you trust Mister Renquist, but have you ever seen the dam? I mean, I know it's not my place, but unless I'm mistaken, you went into this completely sight unseen. I've never heard you question anything he does. Maybe there's more to this than you know."

Banning became quiet as he pondered the situation. "I'm sorry," Meelee said. "I didn't mean to interfere or to cause trouble."

"Meelee, you are a part of this family. You have a perfect right to say anything you feel is necessary. And, now that you've mentioned it, maybe I should look into it further. I'll talk to Adams and Cane in the morning, and I probably should have a look at the dam, as well."

2

I N THE MORNING, CHARGED WITH curiosity, Banning paid
calls on Adams and Cane. The belligerent ways in which he was
received and the answers to his questions about the prices they
paid caused him to move on to other neighbors. From these, he received the same information and, to varying degrees, similar recep-
tions. He promised every person he visited that he would look into
the situation.

He returned to his ranch for some food and was met by Foy's request to accompany him. He refused to allow it, putting Foy into a
pout. Banning decided against addressing his son's attitude at the moment. Instead, he rode into the mountain area known as the Front
Range, following Sorrel Creek to the dam. His observation raised the
possibility that the diversion of the source may have stopped the flow
of water to the neighbors who were now forced to purchase from him
and Renquist. Out of curiosity, he followed the source high into the
mountains to its origin.

As he directed his horse across the rock-laden ground near the
mouth of the waterway, something told him he was not alone. He
was not wrong.

"You should not be here."

The voice from the shadows was deep and spoke as if English was not his primary language. Banning pulled his horse up sharply and froze as he tried to identify the accent.

"This is Cheyenne land," the voice said.

"I—I mean no harm." Banning glanced around as a figure stepped from a bush and approached, brandishing a lance held at the ready. Dressed in the traditional clothing of the Cheyenne, buckskins and moccasins, the man moved cautiously.

"Why you come here?"

As the Cheyenne came closer into his sight, Banning raised his hands to shoulder level, trying to convey a nonthreatening pose. "I was just following the water. My partner and I built a dam downstream. I just wanted to see where the water comes from."

"This one you talk of, this partner, he tall, skinny?"

"Yeah, I guess so." Banning hadn't thought much about how Renquist looked.

"That one promise he pay Cheyenne for water. He not pay. You go back. Tell him pay or we kill him and you."

"I didn't know. I swear I didn't know. I'll settle this and see that you're paid. I promise you. Look, he fooled me too."

"You go. Cheyenne not forget. If no pay soon, we come for you. Pay with life."

Still frozen in place, his heart pounding, Banning did not move.

"Go now!"

Restarted by the Cheyenne's final words, Banning swung his horse around and left the area quickly. He did not slow down until he reached the dam. Then he headed straight for the GR spread.

It was close to dark when Banning rode into the GR ranch house area. Renquist stepped onto the porch and waited. Banning guessed Renquist had seen him approaching. He rode in and pulled rein but remained mounted. The scowl on his face was a message to Renquist that this was not a social call.

"Banning," Renquist said in greeting. His smile was a nervous one.

"Renquist. I want to talk to you." Banning was adamant. "I found out quite a lot today about our water project. There are a lot of questions I want answered."

Renquist's expression did not change. Banning noted that the smile on Renquist's face appeared false. Renquist hesitated, appearing to be thinking quickly. "Whatever it is," he said. "We can discuss it. Why don't you come inside?"

"Never mind that. I'm told we're overcharging for water and now I find out we're violating Cheyenne property rights and withholding payment to them. What the hell are you doing?"

"I can explain everything."

"Go ahead. Explain."

Once again, Renquist hesitated. His face betrayed a search for a way out of this. "Meet me at the dam in the morning. There is something there that will explain this entire situation. You will see."

"I was just there. I saw nothing but the dam."

"It is not something you will see if you are not looking for it. I must show you."

"Tell me about it now."

Again there was hesitation, then Renquist continued, "It is not something so easily explained. You must see it. If we go now, it will be too dark by the time we get there. Just meet me there in the morning and all your questions will be answered."

"Don't take me for a fool, Renquist."

"I swear to you, Banning, I am not. There is nothing going on. We are partners. Everything will be clear to you tomorrow. Please, Banning. Just meet me there."

"We are partners, so this one time I'll give you the benefit of the doubt. What time?"

"Anytime you want. I'll be there waiting for you."

"All right, but this better settle everything."

"It will, Banning, it will."

Banning turned his horse and rode out.

FOY BANNING KNELT BEHIND A bush, transfixed. He knew he saw it, but he was unable to process the event. This was more than his eight-year-old mind could fathom. So, instead, he blocked it out.

He shouldn't be there anyway. Papa's refusal to take him along on this trip to the dam had only made the adventure more enticing. Waiting until Papa was almost out of sight, Foy had quickly saddled his pony and set out to follow at a distance that would keep from his father's sight. When he'd arrived at the location, he carefully hid his mount in a secluded spot and proceeded up the path toward the ridge above the now dry creek bed just forward of the dam. Depositing himself behind a bush that afforded him a clear view of the two men as they stood together on the cliff, he waited and watched to see whatever might occur.

His father stood beside another man Foy recognized as Mr. Renquist. They looked over the cliff at the creek bed below. Their horses were grouped together next to them. Foy watched as words were exchanged between them.

At the same time, Renquist took a step back and reached into the center of the bedroll secured to his saddle. He drew out what appeared to be a metal rod, and with a quick swipe, he struck Foy's father in the back of the head. He watched as his father collapsed and fell over the cliff. Foy's angle of sight and distance did not allow him to see or hear the impact of the body on the rocks below. Renquist leaned slightly over the cliff for a final look.

It was then that Foy knew his father was either badly wounded or dead. And it was then that he blocked the entire incident from his mind. This never happened. His father had not fallen and was not injured. He just couldn't see Papa right then. Foy stared wide-eyed at the scene, his mouth open, a look of horror on his face.

Foy watched as Renquist replaced the bloody instrument into the blanket and walked his horse back to the path leading down from the cliff, leaving Banning's horse where it stood.

Attempting to maintain his cover, Foy moved farther into the bushes, but the sound his movements made drew Renquist's attention as he passed. He dropped his reins and stepped into the brush. Foy watched him walk straight to the hiding place.

"Foy Banning, is that you?"

"Yes, sir." Foy's reply was delayed and hesitant.

Renquist moved closer. "Come out of there, boy. Come here."

Foy stepped out.

"Did you see what just happened?" Renquist asked.

Foy was trembling now. "N—no, sir."

"Are you sure?"

"I didn't see nothing. Papa's going to be real mad I followed him."

Renquist thought for a moment. "Look, boy, there is no easy way to tell you this. Your papa had an accident. He fell over the cliff before I could get to him. I'm afraid he's dead."

Foy took a moment to react. Then he rejected the statement. "Papa can't be dead."

"He is, boy. He fell over. You did not see him land, but I did. He could not have survived that fall."

"Papa can't be dead."

"Come with me. I will take you home."

"Will Papa be there?"

"Listen to me, boy. Your papa is dead. He fell over the cliff. It was an accident. You will not see your papa anymore. Now come with me. I will take you home."

Deep in shock, Foy allowed himself to be led by the hand down to level ground. Renquist found the boy's pony and placed him in the saddle. Taking the reins, Renquist started the trip to the Banning ranch. Throughout the journey, he continually reiterated the story of Banning accidentally falling over the cliff to reinforce Foy's belief in this version.

MEELEE PEERED OUT THE WINDOW of the Banning house in a state of distress. After searching the house and the area surrounding it when she initially realized Foy was missing, her mind now raced to multiple conclusions, none of them good. Finding the boy's pony and saddle gone from the barn, she assumed Banning had taken his son along on the chores of the day. This had occurred in the past, but Banning had always informed her in advance to prevent her from worrying. Today, there was no notice given. Meelee took this as cause for alarm. The images she saw through the window gave her reason to put aside some of her fears, but not all of them. Two riders approached. She readily recognized the smaller figure and the animal on which he rode as Foy and his pony. The boy was safe, or so it appeared. But who was the man with him? It was definitely not Jeremy Banning. She hurried to the front door and stepped out onto the porch for a better look. That did not help. She was forced to await their arrival.

As they drew closer, Grael Renquist came into her view. Renquist held the reins to Foy's pony and led the boy's mount from slightly ahead. That seemed curious. Upon their arrival, the look on Foy's face caused her alarm. It was a look of distance, of not seeming to be present. His eyes were glazed over. This entire image was strange.

Renquist reined in. Foy's pony stopped alongside. Meelee took a step closer.

"Miss Scocroft," Renquist said, almost mechanically. "I'm afraid I must convey some terrible news."

Those words only increased her fears. "What is it? What's happened?" Her voice was agitated.

"You should see to the boy first. He's seen enough already."

Meelee stepped off the porch and went to Foy's side. Whatever this situation turned out to be, her first duty was to protect Foy. "Foy, take Pony to the barn and care for him. He looks tired."

Still exhibiting signs of being in a trance, Foy took the reins from Renquist's extended hand and directed the pony toward the barn. Meelee waited until Foy was out of earshot and then, distraught, turned to Renquist.

"Mister Renquist, please... tell me what happened."

Renquist leaned forward onto the saddlehorn and spoke quietly.

"I'm afraid Mister Banning has met with an accident. We were inspecting the dam, and he fell off a cliff."

Meelee was instantly speechless. She heard his words, but, initially, their full impact did not register in her mind. Standing there, stunned, she tried to process the news as it filtered through her defenses. A tear appeared in her eye and her voice was shaky as she spoke. "I don't understand. You say he's dead?"

"Yes, I'm sure of it."

Then she was full of questions. "How? How did this happen?"

"We were inspecting the dam. He got too close to the edge of the cliff and he fell over. I tried to get to him, but I was too far away. It all happened so quickly. He was gone before I could reach him. He could not have survived that fall. I am sure he's dead."

"Dead." She repeated his last word, still not able to accept the fact.

"I fail to see how a fall like that would not have killed him," Renquist said. "It's got to be forty feet down there. And it is unreachable, so I could not get to him. Unfortunately, what's worse is that I believe the boy saw the whole thing. I found him hiding in the bushes. He said he followed his father and stayed hidden because his father would be angry he had done so. He said he saw nothing, but he could not have missed it, not from where he was. I think he is in shock from the entire experience."

Now awestruck, Meelee uttered a muted, "My God!"

"I'm sorry this happened, Miss Scocroft," Renquist continued. "I did try to save him, but I couldn't. It appears that the boy will need you now more than ever."

"Yes." Meelee's agreement was given absently.

"Please accept my condolences. I must go now and report this to the sheriff."

"Yes." Again there was a lack of presence in her voice.

As Renquist pulled his horse around and rode away quickly, Meelee stared into space for several seconds before concern for Foy overtook her own growing grief and sent her hurrying toward the barn. When she entered, she found Foy curled up in a ball on the floor, sobbing quietly. She hurried to him and scooped him into her arms. Rocking Foy to comfort him, her own loss came forth as tears ran freely down her cheeks.

THE WORDS IN THE TELEGRAM in Charles Banning's hand stunned him. In his second floor office in the Banning Steel Company plant, with factory operations running at full tilt, he leaned back in the desk chair as he stared at the page. It had been almost midday, almost time for lunch, when the messenger had knocked gently on the office door. Over the muffled din of the mill operation, Charles called consent for entry. He received the communication that announced without emotion the death of his brother, Jeremy. It was signed by Darius Cheney, sheriff of Bodeen, Colorado Territory. Briefly, it mentioned that the death had been caused by a fall and gave the date of the incident as several days earlier, June 15, 1865.

Charles and Jeremy were by no means close and had not been for some time. They were, in fact, diametrically opposed in their views of life. They clashed many times over Jeremy's penchant for making his living from the land and Charles's desire to build an industrial empire. Going their separate ways did nothing but separate them further, in distance as well as relationship. Charles had not seen his brother in ten years, had not been present for Jeremy's marriage nor the birth of his son nor the death of his wife. He was too busy to take the time away from his growing domain to re-engage with his estranged brother. Neither, in all that time, had his brother reached out to him. And now the opportunity had been snatched away as if a rug was pulled out from under him. Not that he would have ever acted on that opportunity because of the wall that existed between the two men, but, at least, it had always been available. Now it was gone, as was his brother.

In shock, Charles stared at the words on the page as they burned themselves into his brain. He questioned the efficacy of the estrangement with Jeremy and blamed himself for perpetuating it. A heavy sigh emitted from him as he dropped the document on the desk.

But there were things that must be done now. Jeremy's affairs must be put in order. Provisions had to be made for his son, Foy. These things now fell to Charles to sort out and handle. A trip would need to be made to Colorado straight away. It occurred to him that such a trip would be safer now that the war had ended about a month earlier.

He rose from his chair and trudged to the coat rack, glancing at the same time around the mahogany paneled office and then through the large plate glass window at the factory operations being carried out on the huge manufacturing floor below. This could have been Jeremy's as well. Then, breathing another sigh and stuffing the telegram into his vest pocket, he donned his jacket and derby and left the office.

The taxi driver kept his horse at a trot to quickly cover the several miles across the Youngstown city streets from the mill to the luxurious Banning home located on the north side of the Mahoning River. Charles paid extra for the speed and then hurried up the stone walkway to the front door. Upon entry, he called out in a loud, commanding voice, "Ardith!"

From beyond the top of the staircase in front of him, a mature woman's voice called a reply. "Charles, you're early. We haven't even begun dinner."

"Ardith, come down here, please." There was urgency in his voice.

There was momentary silence before a slim, light haired woman came to the top of the stairs. She was dressed in a prim, high-necked mauve colored dress with lace trim. She started down the steps. "Is something wrong?"

Charles sighed. "Jeremy died." His voice was hushed, with just the hint of emotion. Then, to be perfectly clear, he repeated, "My brother, Jeremy, has died."

The words caught Ardith as she reached the last step. The gravity of his statement jolted her. "Oh, Charles, that's terrible. I'm so sorry."

"I'll have to go to Colorado immediately. Loose ends to be seen to." Now Charles sounded more like the matter-of-fact businessman.

"Of course," Ardith said. "Shall I come with you?"

"That won't be necessary. Rough country out there. Not your cup of tea."

"I'm sure you're right. I'll pack a bag for you." Ardith started back up the stairs and then stopped to look back over her shoulder. "Jeremy had a boy, didn't he? What's to become of him?"

Charles became pensive. "He's one of the loose ends, Ardith. At this point, I have no idea what's to be done with him."

3

THE TWO WEEK TRIP WEST, first by carriage, then by rail, and finally by stagecoach, exhausted Charles. He was unaccustomed to sustained travel and the fractured rest, uncomfortable accommodations and food of indeterminate origin that accompanied it. As the coach rolled into Bodeen, he longed for a good meal and a comfortable bed. Uncertain he would obtain either and equally unsure of what in general to expect in this frontier town, he found himself wringing his hands in anticipation.

Buildings fashioned mostly from clapboard were passed by the coach upon entering Bodeen. Charles scanned these for the office of Sheriff Cheney which was to be his first stop. He identified the location as the coach drove by it and then sat back to wait until the coach reached its depot. He continued to fidget. None of this was by any means pleasant. Accustomed to being in a position of authority, Charles was uncomfortable in situations over which he had little to no control.

The coach pulled to a stop a dozen buildings away from the sheriff's office. At least it was on the same street. Charles and his fellow passengers alighted wearily and collected their luggage from the driver. Carrying the heavy carpet bag, he made his way back up the street, stopping outside the office to catch his breath since exertion was also somewhat of a stranger to him.

As Charles entered, a tall, thin man with a full beard and thinning dark hair turned from the small, wood burning stove in the corner of the room.

Charles placed his bag on the floor. "Sheriff Cheney?"

"That's me." Cheney's voice was firm.

"I'm Charles Banning."

Cheney stepped forward and extended his hand. "Come in, Mister Banning."

Charles stepped closer and shook the sheriff's hand.

"You must be tired from your trip," Cheney said. "Sit down, won't you?"

Accepting the offered chair near the desk, Charles slumped down on it wearily.

Cheney took the seat behind the desk and leaned forward. "You have my condolences, Mister Banning."

"Thank you."

"This must have been a shock for you."

"Yes, it was. Would it be possible to see my brother's body?"

Cheney shook his head in a combination of negativity and distaste. "I'm sorry, but given the condition of the body, we thought it best to—"

"Bury him quickly?"

"Yeah, you know how it is. I can definitely show you where the grave is, though."

"Maybe later. Right now, I'd like to get some answers. How did this happen? Your telegram didn't really say much."

"It was a fall. Him and his partner were up at the dam. He fell over a cliff they were on and landed on the rocks below, must be forty-odd feet down. I don't know if anyone could've survived a fall like that. Took some doing to bring him up from down there."

Charles was surprised at how clinically the lawman related the incident but allowed that one who handles this sort of thing regularly would probably become somewhat jaded in recounting it. His face developed a puzzled look as the sheriff spoke. "I'm confused. I wasn't aware Jeremy had a partner. Is it a partner in his ranch? And what were they doing on that cliff?"

"Reckon you've been out of touch with your brother a while, huh?"

"Jeremy and I have never been close. When he moved out here, we pretty much cut ties altogether."

"Well, near as I can tell, he went into partnership with his neighbor, Grael Renquist, in a water company. They supply water to the land owners hereabouts. They went up to the cliff to check that the dam was holding sound, so Renquist tells me. Your brother got too close to the edge. He fell over before Renquist could reach him. Renquist come and got me right off, but there was nothing anybody could do. Jeremy was dead when we got him up from the rocks. Likely died from the impact of hitting them."

"I see," Charles said simply.

The sheriff cleared his throat. "Reckon you're finding out a heap you didn't know about your brother."

Charles shook his head in astonishment. "Yes, I am. And it's only made me more curious. Is there anything else you can tell me?"

Cheney scrunched his face in a look that betrayed vague suspicions. He thought for a moment before he spoke. "Not really, 'cepting I just found it a mite strange that Jeremy would allow himself to get so close to the edge of that cliff. I didn't know him that well but he always struck me as being level-headed, not one to put himself in a dangerous spot like that if he could help it… if you take my meaning."

Charles took up the thought with interest. "Sheriff, are you saying my brother died under... questionable circumstances?"

"Not saying anything of the kind. I just found it a mite strange is all. Then again, everybody makes mistakes now and again and I've seen stranger things than that in my time."

THE BUGGY CARRYING CHARLES AND his hired driver made its way to the cemetery outside the Bodeen town limits and came to a stop on the road near the entrance. Supplied with location instructions he'd obtained from the undertaker, Charles alighted and walked to the grave, hat in hand.

The modest wooden marker with rounded top and carved lettering stood at the head of the still freshly covered grave. It identified the remains within as those of Jeremy Banning, along with the date and cause of his death. Charles stopped there to allow the scene to flow into his memory. This was precious little to show for a life Jeremy loved so much. Standing there, Charles silently delivered the obligatory farewell, lingered a few moments and then returned to the carriage.

The journey to the Banning ranch brought him into rougher country. It only added to his opinion that his brother had no business living here when he could have existed much more comfortably back in Youngstown. Charles resolved then and there that Jeremy's son would have a better chance at life than his father allowed. Indeed, Jeremy's wife might even be alive today and so might he.

With the driver having been chosen by Sheriff Cheney for his knowledge of the area, Charles was taken on a direct route to the Banning home. As they approached the location, he watched as a young woman left the house and crossed the front yard toward a child who stood at the corral fence. The woman call the boy's name.

The boy did not answer or acknowledge the call. He simply stood at the corral staring into space. Catching sight of the approaching buggy, the woman changed direction and moved toward it. As the conveyance drew to a halt, she came alongside.

Charles removed his hat. Unaware of the woman's function here, he dealt with her formally. "Good day, miss. Charles Banning, Jeremy's brother."

Meelee appeared to become unsettled by his approach, but she forced a smile. "Oh, Mister Banning. How do you do. I'm so... please accept my... I can't tell you how sorry I am about your brother."

"Thank you. And you are?"

"Amelia Scocroft. I cared for Jeremy's wife until she passed. Now I look after Foy."

Charles looked beyond her to the small boy at the corral. "I take it that's Foy there?"

"Yes."

Charles stepped out of the buggy and walked tentatively toward the boy. Having never met his brother's son and lacking the skill to communicate with someone so young, he slowed as he drew nearer, his mind racing for an answer to how this should be handled.

Finally settling on treating him as an equal, he continued to the boy's side. "How do you do, Foy? I'm your Uncle Charles."

The words fell on uninterested ears. Foy continued to stare ahead. Charles, experiencing inadequacy, placed a hand on Foy's shoulder and felt him tense slightly. "I'm here to help you, Foy. Your father and I were not close, but that has nothing to do with you and me. I can never take your father's place, but I can do everything necessary to help you through this difficult time if you'll let me."

Foy said nothing. He relaxed slightly under Charles's hand, but he remained silent.

"Foy?" Charles said tentatively.

After a second, Foy turned and hugged Charles's body, appearing to reach out for comfort. Charles placed his hands on the boy's back and drew him close, holding him for as long as Foy needed to stay there. Touched by Foy's silent expression of his needs, Charles gave himself to the situation. Never having been a parent, this was new territory for him, but he allowed himself to become immersed in the emotion of the moment.

Several minutes passed while Foy hung on to Charles's body dearly. When Charles felt the boy release, he held Foy back a little and, with some effort, crouched down to be on his level.

"We're going to work this out, Foy," Charles whispered. "We're going to work it out."

"Papa's gone." The boy's eyes were wet with tears. They ran down his cheeks in dusty little trails and fell on his shirt.

Charles pulled him into a hug. "I know, son, but I'm here now. It's going to be all right."

Foy settled down a few minutes later. Meelee joined them and suggested the boy go to the barn and care for his pony.

Foy obeyed the request and headed for the barn. Meelee and Charles walked slowly toward the house.

"I'm glad you came," Meelee said. "That's the first time since Jeremy died that Foy has reacted at all. Until now, he's just stared off into nothing."

"My brother and I weren't close, but the boy seems okay with me."

"You're family. He can tell that. It makes a difference."

Charles stopped and turned to face Meelee. "Miss Scocroft, I was not aware of your residence here. How long has it been?"

"It's nearly three years now. Jeremy hired me to care for his wife when she became ill. He found it impossible to take care of her and Foy and to look after the ranch at the same time. After she passed, he asked me to stay on to help raise Foy. Why do you ask?"

"Well, I'm trying to decide what would be best for Foy. My first thought is to take him back to Ohio with me so my wife and I can provide for him. But I hesitate to uproot him after what he's been through here. How close is he to you?"

"We are close, but truth be told, we're not family. I do love Foy and I want only what's best for him. If you feel it best to take him with you, away from here, then, of course, you should do that. And, I believe he'd definitely have better opportunities with you. But, may I suggest that you ask him first? He's been through a great deal, but he knows his own mind. If you try to impose your will on him, I think he might resist."

Charles considered for a moment. "I take your point."

"We can discuss it over dinner. Will you stay?"

Charles smiled. "Yes, I'd like that."

MEELEE PREPARED A QUICK MEAL that consisted of baked chicken and greens. The dinner table was host to a discussion of the point which Charles saw as most important, that being Foy's future. Charles's suggestion that Foy return with him to Ohio to live with him and Ardith met with initially with lukewarm reception. Foy was reluctant to leave Meelee and his pony and the home he had known since birth. The exchange that followed gently convinced the boy that leaving Colorado was in his best interests. He did not consent, however, before exacting a promise from Charles to have the pony shipped to Ohio so he could continue to raise it. He also secured a commitment from Meelee to come east to visit when she could. Charles found himself admiring Foy's bargaining abilities.

As soon as Foy was put to bed, Charles and Meelee stepped onto the porch to discuss an item that had not been raised until this point.

"I want you to know I'm not going to hold you to that trip to Ohio. I've learned firsthand the difficulties involved in that. But, if you do decide to come, I'll cover your expenses. In addition to that, since you will soon become unemployed, I'd like to offer you severance. What would you say to a year's salary?"

Meelee seemed surprised by Charles's generosity. "You have no idea how much Jeremy paid me. I could tell you anything."

Charles smiled at her. He was surprised at his own level of trust in this stranger. It seemed to him that his new connection with the boy had unleashed some hidden traits he was not aware he possessed. "I trust you. After all, you didn't have to remain after Jeremy's death. You could have left when your salary stopped. I'm sure you did that out of concern for Foy. You deserve to be compensated for that."

"You're very kind, sir. Since I'm not in a position to refuse, I accept your offer. But I insist upon paying my own expenses if I do come to visit Foy."

"We can discuss that when it arises. For now, just give me the amount Jeremy paid you. I have a letter of credit drawn on my bank in Youngstown. I can write you a draft against it. You can cash it at the bank in Bodeen."

"Well... he paid me seven dollars a week. In addition to that, I also lived here and took all my meals here. I couldn't begin to put a figure to all that.

"Then we'll just double it. Let's see... fifteen a week... sixty a month... seven-twenty... how does an even eight hundred sound?"

"That's more than generous, Mister Banning, but really, you shouldn't—"

"Yes, Miss Scocroft, I should. To show my appreciation for what you've done for Foy, and, I think, for Jeremy as well, yes, I definitely should. Now, if you have pen and ink...."

4

CHARLES RETURNED TO BODEEN LATE that night. He paid the driver, took his travel bag from the buggy and went to the hotel to rent a room. There he settled in for a rather uncomfortable rest. These were not exactly luxury accommodations. The room was sparse and in need of painting. It had one small window with glass so dirt-encrusted that seeing out was made difficult. The bed was hard and lumpy and the chest of drawers was cheap and ill-fitted. It was about what he expected in a town this size. Sleep was unpleasant and almost nonexistent.

In the morning, he consumed a bacon and egg breakfast at the local restaurant and moved on to the bank to investigate his brother's holdings. Finding the paltry amount in Jeremy's savings insignificant, he requested those funds to be combined with the meager sum in Foy's business account. He then gave the banker instructions for transferring both to Charles's own bank in Youngstown to be held in an escrow account until he returned. Further, he commissioned the banker to act as his agent to sell the Banning property and assets to the highest bidder and to forward those moneys, minus an agreed service fee, to the same account in Youngstown. Finally, after reviewing the Renquist & Banning Water Co. partnership agreement, he decided he wanted no part of a long distance management situation. He allowed Jeremy's interest in that to revert to the surviving partner.

Following this lengthy conference, Charles verified the stagecoach schedule and then reengaged his buggy driver. They set out again for the Banning ranch, arriving close to lunch time. Meelee responded to the knock on the door and admitted him.

"Good day, Miss Scocroft," Charles said as he entered. "I've taken care of all of Jeremy's affairs this morning. I'm here now to collect Foy."

"I—I didn't expect it would be so soon," she said in a tentative voice. "I haven't packed any of his things or gotten him ready."

"There's plenty of time for that. The coach doesn't leave until four this afternoon."

"If you don't mind, I'd like him to have lunch first."

"Of course. May I join you?"

"Please. I think he'd like that."

Charles detected a hesitation in Meelee's manner and decided to address it. "Miss Scocroft, I understand your reluctance, but you must agree that this is best for him."

"I do, Mister Banning, of course." She seemed to speak sincerely. "I'm thankful that you're here, but that doesn't make this any easier. Foy is special to me and I'll miss him dearly. And, as well, I'm having trouble accepting that I'll be alone now." Meelee's voice cracked as she finished her statement and a tear escaped her eye.

Charles noted this. "I know this must be difficult for you, but I'm sure you'll have no trouble finding another situation. You would be a credit to any employer."

Meelee used a handkerchief to wipe away the tears. "Thank you. I just have to convince myself of that."

Charles smiled. "I think you've done an exceptional job. Foy's a fine young man. May I go to him now and help him prepare to leave?"

"Of course. He's in the barn."

Charles nodded as his smile broadened. "With his pony, of course."

Charles entered the barn and stopped. Foy stood beside his pony in the center of the building, his back to the entrance. The boy worked a dandy brush in short arcs across the animal's back. Charles noted that this was probably the last grooming session there would be until the two were reunited in Ohio. He understood that Foy believed this bonding gesture would strengthen the young horse's memory of its master.

"Uncle Charles promised to bring you to Ohio for me," Foy said softly to the pony. "But I don't know how long that will be, so don't you forget me, you hear?"

"I'm sure he'll remember you." Charles spoke from the barn entrance. Foy turned his head upon hearing his uncle's voice. Charles approached as he continued. "I know I would if you treated me like that."

"He looks fine, don't he?" Foy's smile was one of pride in a job well done.

"He does for a fact." Charles stopped at Foy's side. "Now, I'd like you to go up to the house and eat lunch. We're leaving for Ohio this afternoon, so you'll need to get your things packed." Charles went to a knee to equal Foy's height. "But I promise you, before we leave, we'll arrange for the pony to be shipped. You and I, we'll make those arrangements together. Then you'll know he'll be well treated. I'm sure it won't be long before he arrives in Youngstown and is back with you."

Foy tried to sustain his smile but was only able to emit a heavy sigh.

"What is it?" Charles asked.

"I'm sad to leave Meelee. I'll miss her."

"I know, son, but, sadly, I can't bring her with us. I'm afraid she would have to start over in a strange place and that would be hard for her. I can assure you that Meelee will be well taken care of. I've seen to that. And I've also told her that when she comes to visit you, she doesn't have to be concerned with money. Does that make you feel any better?"

Foy sighed again. "I guess so."

"Well, that's good. Now, can we go on up to the house?"

Charles took the brush from Foy's hand and put it aside. Together, they put Pony back in its stall and closed the gate. Charles took the boy's hand and led him out of the barn. They walked slowly toward the house.

After lunch, Charles and Meelee helped Foy pack his traveling bag. Foy placed it in the buggy. After tying the pony to the back, Charles and Foy boarded the carriage and set out for Bodeen. Meelee followed, driving the Banning buckboard.

Upon arrival, Charles and Foy led Pony to the local stable. Charles made arrangements with the owner to ship Pony, stressing the preferential treatment that was required and stressing that price was not a factor. Foy was satisfied and the deal was made. Foy spent a few emotional moments saying goodbye and left with tears in his eyes. As they walked to the stagecoach depot where Meelee waited for them, Foy sniffled back his sad feelings.

Outside the depot building, they waited for the arrival of the coach. Foy found a piece of wood and began whittling with his pocket knife as Meelee spoke with Charles.

"As soon as you leave, I'll go back to the ranch and clear out my belongings."

Charles raised his hand in a halting gesture. "There's no rush for that. I have no objection to your staying on until the property is sold. And, please feel free to keep the wagon. You'll need it to transport your things."

Meelee smiled. "You've been so kind. Perhaps I shouldn't say this, but I can't fathom why you and Jeremy were not closer. You're so much alike."

Charles nodded knowingly. "Alike and different at the same time. There were major differences between us. I wish it were not so, but I'm afraid it's too late to rectify them now. Funny, they don't seem so significant now."

"I'm sorry."

Charles did not reply to that. He merely flashed a frown and shook his head. They waited in silence after that.

The coach made its appearance a few minutes later, generating activity among the waiting passengers. Their luggage was secured and goodbyes were begun. Foy closed his knife and ran to Meelee's open arms. Their hug lasted at least a minute and became tearful on both their parts. Charles put his hand on Foy's shoulder to indicate the time to leave had come.

"I'll miss you, Meelee," Foy said through his sobs. "You have to come visit."

"I'll try, Foy, I'll really try."

Reluctantly, Foy leaned back and allowed Charles to lift him into the coach.

Charles turned to Meelee and extended his hand. "Goodbye, Miss Scocroft, it's been a distinct pleasure."

Meelee shook his hand. "Thank you, Mister Banning, for everything. I will try to visit."

"You'll always be welcome."

Charles stepped aboard the coach. The driver whipped up the team and drove the conveyance up the street. Foy leaned out the open window and waved vigorously back at Meelee who, tearfully, responded in kind.

"Bye, Meelee," Foy shouted. "Bye!"

5

ECEIVED WITH OPEN ARMS AND nurtured lovingly by his Aunt Ardith, while being mentored by a changed Charles, Foy adapted quickly to his new life. When the pony arrived, he helped Charles arrange for its boarding at a local stable and resumed his relationship with the animal. That served to heal some of the boy's emotional wounds.

As he gradually accepted the permanent loss of his father, the only empty spot in Foy's life remained the absence of Meelee. Soon, as he settled into a new, more formal school life in a prestigious academy and continued to fill his time with riding and caring for the pony, the heartache of separation began to wane and Meelee faded into just a memory.

Several months into Foy's new existence, Charles received a letter from Meelee. After reading it, he sat alone pondering a question the letter raised for him. Ardith, noticing his preoccupation, took the seat next to him on the couch.

"What is it, Charles? You seem distressed."

"It's this letter that came today. It's from Miss Scocroft."

"Oh, is she coming to visit? That would be lovely. Why would that upset you?"

"Actually, it's just the opposite. She writes that she's met a man and is planning to marry him. Because of that, she doesn't feel she'll be able to visit. She also asks if we think it best for her to allow her relationship with Foy to—I don't know—fade away, as she puts it. She expects the marriage to take all of her time and wonders if it's fair to Foy to continue corresponding with him, knowing that she'll probably never see him again. I honestly am at a loss as to how to handle this. What are your thoughts?"

Ardith seemed to grasp the gravity of the situation and gave it deep thought before answering. "Foy hardly speaks of her anymore. I can't remember the last time he wrote to her. Perhaps, if she stops writing, she'll just become a distant memory to him. That might be best for the both of them."

"I think you're right. I'll write back to her and tell her that. I'm sure she'll understand."

After Charles's reply letter reached her, Meelee never again contacted Foy.

FOUR YEARS PASSED, YEARS THAT saw Foy excel in his studies at the private school he attended. As he moved on to higher education, it became clear that his aptitude lay not in business, which disappointed Charles as he sought to groom Foy as heir to the steel mill. Instead, Foy was drawn to the field of medicine.

Several times, during sporting events in which he engaged, Foy found himself in the center of medical emergencies involving his fellow students. His responses to those events not only made his talent apparent, but they demonstrated his willingness to apply it. "I've been reading about these things. I can help."

When Charles questioned him regarding his career, Foy enthusiastically indicated his desire to become a doctor. Wanting only what was best for Foy, Charles began immediate preparations for Foy's admission to a medical college. With Foy's involvement, the choice was made to apply to the Medical Department of the University of the Pacific in Santa Clara, California. Just prior to graduating his current school, and shortly after submitting his application, Foy was accepted to the college. After graduation, he prepared to move to California.

ARDITH WATCHED EIGHTEEN-YEAR-OLD Foy come down the stairs from his room. He was no longer the towheaded little boy Charles had brought back from Colorado ten years earlier. He had become a tall, slim, handsome young man who carried himself proudly. As he reached the last step and set his carpetbag down in front of him, he smiled at his aunt.

"I'm so proud of you, but I really hate to see you leave."

"I hate that part of it, too, leaving you and Uncle Charles, but it's not forever. I'll write every week if I can, and I'm looking forward to you coming to visit me in the summer."

"I know. It's just I've gotten so used to you being here that—" Ardith's statement was interrupted by the front door opening.

Charles stepped in, speaking as he walked. "Foy, are you ready? The cab is here."

"I'm ready." Foy reached to pick up his luggage and then turned to Ardith who, by now, was wiping a tear from her eye.

"Aunt Ardith," he said softly. "Please don't be sad. This is the chance I've been waiting for. It won't be very long before you can come visit for the summer."

"I know, dear," Ardith's voice cracked as she spoke. "I'll just have to bear it." She pulled Foy down to her level and placed a soft kiss on his forehead. "Be careful."

In response, he put his arm around her and embraced her and then turned to Charles. "Will you see that Pony is cared for?"

"Of course. You take care of yourself, Foy."

"I will. I'm going to stop in Bodeen to visit Papa's grave."

"I know he'd like that."

Charles and Foy shook hands. Foy went to the open door and walked out to the waiting cab. The Bannings watched as the boy left to begin the next phase of his young life.

6

THE YEAR WAS 1875 AND developments in the ability to travel made Foy's trip west considerably faster than the original journey had been for him and Charles ten years earlier. The railroad had now reached far enough west to make it possible to go from Youngstown to Denver completely by train. Although he was weary as the train pulled to a stop at the Denver station, Foy found comfort in the elimination of the need to ride stagecoaches.

In Denver, he rented a horse and saddle and started south from Denver to Bodeen, the streets of which he had not seen in ten years. He secured general directions from the stableman and, as he rode through the mountainous terrain toward the town, the memories of this land rushed back to him. Along with this came the twinge of a faded recollection, an incident in the mountains long ago. As quickly as it sprung up, that was how fast it disappeared, leaving him with uncertain questions and no clear answers or memories. It occurred to him that maybe it never actually happened. He dismissed it as a nagging nostalgia brought on by familiar surroundings.

His entry into Bodeen by the main street generated another rush of memories from his youth. The town had changed since he was last here. It had grown in size, sporting new buildings next to older structures, newer businesses where he remembered others had been. These stood alongside establishments that had endured and were quite recognizable to him.

He directed his horse to the hitch rail outside the hotel and dismounted rather heavily. It had been quite a while since he had ridden a great distance. His jaunts at home, on Pony, were never more than a few miles. The nagging ache in his back reminded him of this.

Releasing his carpet bag from behind the saddle tie, he mounted the steps to the boardwalk. Deep in his own thoughts, he paid no attention to passersby around him and promptly collided with a young woman carrying packages as she strode at right angles to him. A minor encounter, it did no more than upset her parcels and cause her to drop several. Pulled back to reality, Foy fumbled to catch her to prevent her from falling, grabbing her arm clumsily and voicing a makeshift apology for his lack of vigilance. "I'm sorry, ma'am. That was awfully dumb of me."

The woman recovered quickly. Foy released her arm as soon as he was certain she would not falter.

"It's all right," she said. "No harm done."

He flashed an embarrassed smile and stooped to retrieve her packages. When he had placed them back in her arms, he tipped his hat. She smiled back, but she studied him for a second before moving on. As he reached to open the hotel's door, he looked again at the woman. There was something very familiar about her. He wondered if he'd seen her before. He chalked it up to his prior acquaintance with the town and allowed that he might have seen her on one of his trips to town with his father. Dismissing it, he stepped into the hotel lobby.

A quick dinner, an uncomfortable night's sleep, and an equally unpalatable breakfast followed his registration. Retrieving his horse from the stable at which he had lodged it the previous night, he saddled up and rode to the cemetery outside the town. The layout of the area had changed somewhat since he was here as an eight-year-old but he managed to search out the plot in which his father had been laid to rest. While the wooden marker had endured the weathering ten years of exposure had dealt, the grave itself exhibited recent care. He found that curious. The surrounding graves were in various states of care, some pristine, most overgrown with grass and weeds. This discounted the possibility that all graves here were cared for. More than likely someone had concentrated on this one. But who?

Approaching the grave slowly, he removed his hat and stopped at the foot. There he stood quietly reflecting. A renewed sense of loss, which had waned over the years, flooded his being. He uttered a silent prayer and then simply stared aimlessly at the marker for an uncounted amount of time.

"You *are* Foy Banning, aren't you?" The woman's voice was behind him.

Recognizing the voice from the day before, Foy turned sharply to see the woman with whom he had collided in town. She was in a simple but flattering dress very similar to the one she wore the previous day. More recollections crowded into his mind as the identity of this woman became clear to him. "Meelee?"

She smiled broadly and nodded.

"Oh, my God," he said in surprise. "Meelee."

Instinctively, his arms went out to her. Just as instinctively, she moved to him and embraced him warmly. He responded in kind. Taller now than she was, he nestled her against his chest in a similar fashion to the embraces she had provided him when he was a child. They remained that way for several seconds.

"I thought that was you yesterday," she said as she stepped back. "But I wasn't sure. Seeing you here convinced me."

Foy regarded her, grinning. "I thought I'd never see you again. How are you?"

"I'm well." She looked at him and smiled broadly. "I can't believe how you've grown. Jeremy always said you'd be tall. I see now he was right."

"I guess he was."

"We have to talk, to catch up. How long will you be here?"

"I'm just passing through. I'm on my way to California to start medical school in the fall. I wanted to stop by Papa's grave."

"Medical school! Oh, Foy, that's wonderful. I'm so proud of you."

Foy's grin broadened. "I haven't done anything yet."

"I'm sure you'll make an excellent doctor." Meelee's hand went to his arm. "Oh, please, stay at least long enough for us to catch up over dinner, won't you?"

"Yes, I'd like that. It's been so long. So much has happened. Shall we say tonight?"

"Of course. There's a decent restaurant in town called Cafe Pierre. It's right near the hotel. Seven o'clock?"

Foy nodded vigorously. "Yes, I'll be there."

"Wonderful. Now I have to hurry. I usually stop here once a week on my way to work to see that everything is in order."

"You've been taking care of Papa's grave all these years?"

"Why, yes. It's the least I can do."

"Meelee, there's so much I want to ask you."

"I know, Foy, and there's so much I want to tell you. We'll talk at dinner."

EVENING FOUND FOY AT THE door of the restaurant, dressed

in a dark suit and homburg. He paused momentarily at the entrance and glanced over his shoulder to see Meelee approaching along the boardwalk. She had changed her attire from the obvious work related garment she had worn earlier to a more formal one. A matching hat and umbrella completed her outfit. Foy took a moment to absorb the vision. He had forgotten and, as a boy, had not appreciated, the beautiful woman Amelia Scocroft had always been.

"Well, good evening, Miss Scocroft."

"Good evening, *Mister* Banning." She curtsied primly.

He offered his arm and she placed her hand in the crook as he opened the door and ushered her inside to an unoccupied table. He pulled a chair out and seated her. She smiled at him as he dropped his hat on an unoccupied chair and took a seat across from her. A waiter arrived, greeted them and handed each of them a menu. Foy glanced at the page.

"What's good here?"

"The *coq au vin* is very good."

"Then that's what it'll be. And for you?"

"The same."

Foy placed the menus aside.

"It's so good to see you." Meelee reached out to touch his hand. "I really missed you."

Foy frowned. "I don't mean to sound harsh, but why did you stop writing? Why didn't you come to Ohio? You promised you would."

Meelee's other hand came to rest on Foy's. "I'm really sorry I couldn't come. Shortly after you left with your uncle, I met someone. I guess the loss of your father left me more vulnerable than I realized. I fell into what I thought was love with this man. I wrote to your uncle and told him it would not be possible for me to visit. I asked him how I should handle it with you. His advice was to do nothing and let your memory of me fade away. It hurt me to do that, but he thought it best."

Foy took a second to digest this revelation. "He never said anything to me about that. I can't imagine what his reasoning was, but I guess, over time, I forgot. Did you marry the man you met?"

"Almost. I found out just before we were to be married that he was trying to swindle me out of what little money I had. I was so angry, I ran him off. I literally took a gun to him."

"You shot him?" Foy's words and expression showed amazement.

Meelee chuckled. "No, but he thought I would, so he ran for his life."

Foy grinned. "That's the Meelee I remember." As he spoke, he laid his free hand on top of hers. Her smile broadened.

"After he left," Meelee said. "I was so embarrassed that I just withdrew into myself. I never became involved with anyone again and I never contacted Charles again. In truth, I became that dried-up old spinster they write books about."

"You certainly don't look like that to me." Foy looked deeply into her eyes and began to understand something he had observed as a child but paid no heed to back then. "You loved Papa, didn't you?"

Her expression turned serious. "Yes, Foy, yes, I did."

"Why didn't you ever say anything to him? I'm sure he felt the same about you."

"It was very complicated. He was still grieving over the loss of your mother. There just never seemed to be a right time to bring it up. And I was always concerned that it would look like I was taking advantage of him. I don't know, it was just very difficult—" Her voice cracked as she stopped in mid-sentence.

Foy squeezed her hands to show support. "I'm sorry it never worked out for you. You deserved much better than that. I understand now. I never realized why his death affected you so much. Now I do."

Meelee blinked her eyes to allay tears. "It was more than just his death. It was the way he died." She hesitated for a second, then the floodgates opened. "I couldn't believe it was an accident. He might have been too trusting, but he wasn't that careless. He left that morning without telling me where he was going. He never did that. Then, when you went missing, I was beside myself. When Renquist brought you home and told me Jeremy had fallen off that cliff, I was devastated. I channeled that into consoling you. It didn't dawn on me until later that Renquist's story sounded somehow false to me. I didn't think I should say anything about it because I had nothing to support it. It was merely a suspicion."

Foy showed deep interest. It started him thinking. "You know, there is something strange about that morning. Something happened, but… I just…." He shook his head. "I can't remember it. I think it might have had something to do with Papa. I wish I could remember."

"Foy, do you think there's a possibility Renquist had something to do with Jeremy's death?"

"I don't know. I guess it's possible. Maybe we should look into it, maybe talk to the sheriff."

"Unfortunately, Bodeen doesn't have a sheriff anymore. When Sheriff Cheney retired, the council decided to have the Denver sheriff's office police the town to save money."

"Is Sheriff Cheney still here? Maybe he can remember something."

"He came down with consumption a while ago. He's in a sanatorium now, up in Denver somewhere. People who were close to him say he's dying."

Foy was motivated now. "That's too bad, but maybe his files are still here. I know his office is still there. I passed it when I rode in. Maybe we can go through the files, see if we can, I don't know, come up with something."

"You might be right, but the council keeps the office locked. We'd have to get the key from them."

Foy was more excited now. "Meelee, I'd like to try. Are you free tomorrow morning?"

"I can be."

"Will you meet me at the hotel at eight o'clock? We can try to get that key."

"Yes, Foy, I'll meet you."

As Foy and Meelee continued their conversation, Grael Renquist, ten years older, but not much changed, sat alone, unnoticed, at a corner table in the back of the restaurant. He viewed with interest the meeting between Amelia Scocroft and this unknown young man.

7

RENQUIST REMAINED SECRETED AT HIS corner table carefully watching Meelee and Foy. Aware that his location kept him out of their view, he waited to keep them from seeing him and he was curious as to how long they remained and talked. He sat through his own meal as well as theirs and continued to scrutinize them until they rose and left the restaurant. Then he hung back an additional few minutes to be certain Meelee and the young man would not see him. Only then did Renquist exit. He hurried straight for the saloon across the street.

As he pushed through the batwings, his eyes scanned the crowded barroom and settled on Brent Talkot, a tall, burly individual in traditional cowhand work clothes who occupied a space at the bar among other, similarly dressed men. Renquist made his way to the man and touched his arm to gain his attention. "Brent."

The big man turned. He was wide in build with powerful arms and chest and just the hint of a belly. His face was large with expressive features and a dark complexion.

"Come with me," Renquist said.

Both men separated from the group and moved to an obscure corner of the place.

"I need you to do something for me," Renquist said.

"Sure, boss." Talkot's voice was a deep baritone.

"There's a stranger in town, a young man. I just now observed him dining with Amelia Scocroft, the woman from the boarding house. He seems familiar to me. I want you to find out who he is."

Talkot seemed annoyed. "Why don't you just go ask him yourself?"

"I have my reasons. Start with the hotel. He's probably registered there. Talk to the clerk. See if someone named Banning is staying there. Verify with him that it's a young man, tall with hair the color of sand. Do this tonight before you leave town."

"Tonight? We ain't done celebrating yet."

"You are now. Find this out and bring me the answer straight away. I'll be at home."

Reluctance tinged Talkot's voice. "Yeah, sure."

Renquist stared at him for a moment, then turned and went toward the door. As he mounted his horse, which had been tied at the hitch rail outside the restaurant, he saw Talkot leave the saloon. He watched pointedly as the big man walked heavily up the street toward the hotel. Then Renquist turned his horse and rode off in the opposite direction.

RENQUIST CHEWED ON A CIGAR that was no longer burning. He paced the expanse of his parlor awaiting the arrival of his foreman and the delivery of the information Talkot was charged with gathering. If this young man turned out to be Banning's son, and if he decided to stay on in Bodeen, this would need to be dealt with. Trying to contain his anxiety until it was warranted, he expended his nervous energy on the cigar and the parlor rug.

The knock on the front door moved him quickly to admit Talkot. "What have you learned?"

Talkot stepped into the foyer. "You were right about him staying at the hotel. Room number seven. Banning's his name, all right. Foy Banning. He signed the register yesterday."

Renquist chewed the cigar some more and paced briefly. This facilitated his ability to think. He turned to face Talkot, his intensity increased tenfold. "I want you to follow him. Wherever he goes, you go. Stay out of sight, but stay on him. I want to know where he goes and who he sees. If you can get close enough without being seen, listen to his conversations and report back to me."

Talkot hesitated. Then he spoke up. "Hey, I got a lot of stuff going on with the ranch. I ain't got the time to do that shit. You ought to get somebody else—"

Renquist cut him off. "You work for *me*, Brent. You will do what I tell you, whatever I tell you. I want no one else involved in this. Delegate whatever needs to be done here to others. I don't care what you have to do, but I want this done and done only by you. This is vital to me. Do you understand?"

Again, Talkot hesitated. Renquist's determined stare won out. Talkot seemed to grasp the need to acquiesce.

"I savvy. But I don't like spying on folks."

Renquist pressed his point. "What you like or dislike is of no interest to me. If you value your place here, you'll do as I say without question or comment."

"All right, all right! Give me a few minutes to set things up here, then I'll get on it."

Renquist settled down. "That's better. Remember, though—don't let him see you. I want to know everything he does. *Everything*. Do you hear?"

Talkot now appeared to be resigned to the assignment. "Yeah, I hear you."

Renquist held out an incentive. "Handle this well and you'll be equally rewarded."

Talkot still appeared reluctant. "Yeah, I'll figure it out."

Talkot left the house without another word. Renquist returned to pacing and cigar chomping. This small accomplishment of forcing Talkot to do his bidding did not allay his concerns. Only answers to his questions would do that.

―――――――

AT TEN OF EIGHT THE next morning, Foy stepped through the hotel doorway and waited on the boardwalk. Within a few minutes, Meelee approached him. As she walked, she passed the alley beside the hotel. A burly man in the alley leaned against the wall, smoking a cigarette. She paid him no heed.

"Good morning," Foy said as she reached him.

"Foy, this could be opening old wounds again for you," she said. "Are you sure you want to go through with this?"

"Yes, I'm sure."

"Then let's go."

Meelee led the way to the court house at the edge of town, bringing Foy up to date on the shape of Bodeen's government in the ten years he'd been away.

"When they did away with the sheriff's position, the mayor and the full-time council was eliminated, as well. Now, we have Mister Pelley, the justice-of-the-peace. He also acts as mayor and head of the council."

They sought out Mr. Pelley who was reluctant to surrender the key to the sheriff's office and jail "...to just anyone that asks."

"My name is Foy Banning. I have a good reason for asking, sir." He and Meelee stood in the court house facing Mr. Pelley. "Ten years ago, my father, Jeremy Banning, died in what was termed an accident."

Pelley thought as Foy spoke. "Oh, yeah," Pelley said in a snarling, elderly voice. "I remember that. Nasty accident, as I recollect."

Foy continued. "I was too young to ask questions back then. I'd like to go over the sheriff's records to satisfy myself that there were no improprieties in the case."

Pelley became defensive. "You don't need to see the records to put that to rest. I can tell you, I was there. Everything was done by the book."

"With all due respect, sir, I've come all the way from Ohio to do this. Please allow it."

Meelee broke in gently. "Mister Pelley, those are public records, are they not?"

"Yes, Miss Scocroft, they are."

"Then there should be no reason to deny this. Foy is simply trying to answer questions that have frustrated him for the last ten years."

"I suppose...."

Foy offered a further argument. "Seeing the records would help me move on with my life. You know, losing a parent is hard enough, but when it's under questionable circumstances—"

"Now, just a minute, young man. I told you everything was on the up-an-up—"

Foy pressed it home. "Then allow me to see that for myself. Examining those records should only take a few minutes. If, as you say, everything was done correctly, I'll return the key, and you'll never hear from me again."

"Well, I guess it can't hurt none." The old man dug into his vest pocket and brought out the key. "I'll be right here. See you bring that back promptly," he said as he handed out the key.

Foy took the key. "Absolutely."

Meelee smiled at Pelley. She joined Foy and they left the court-house. They walked quickly to the jail, opened the padlock and en-tered. Stagnant air trapped inside, the result of months of closure, greeted them, taking their breath away momentarily. Foy raised a window sash to remedy the situation. They looked around the sparse, dust-covered office.

Meelee sniffed. "It looks like nobody's cleaned this place since Sheriff Cheney left."

"Probably true." Foy focused on the point of interest. "Just one cabinet. Should make it fairly easy."

He started at the top drawer of the four tier cabinet, attempting to determine the method of filing that was used. Quickly, he found that the sheriff's system had the earliest cases in the lower drawers and that each file was identified by the name of the victim. It took only a few minutes to locate the file in question.

Several pages bearing dated handwritten entries described the sheriff's first contact with the case. Grael Renquist notified him of the death of his partner, Jeremy Banning. Subsequent notations showed the discovery of the body on the rocks below the cliff at the Sor-rel Creek Dam. An account of the victim's injuries was particularly graphic, causing Foy to be repelled momentarily as he read through the report.

Foy held the documents so that Meelee could see, allowing her to read along with him. A pained expression crossed his face as he went over the details of the various wounds sustained by his father. Meelee displayed a similar reaction.

"If you notice here, the sheriff mentions a specific wound." Foy pointed to the passage and read the sheriff's exact words aloud, "Wound in the back of the victim's head is suspicious. I tend to doubt it could have been caused by the fall because the body landed flat on its front with no damage to its back, except for that one gash."

Further into the file, they found the coroner's report, attributing death to the fall and ruling it an accident. The sheriff's notes later on discounted his suspicions of the head wound, deferring to the coroner's expertise. The case was closed with no further action warranted and was signed by Darius Cheney, Sheriff.

"It looks like I wan't the only one who thought there was something suspicious about this," Meelee said. "I wish I'd have known about this back then. I would have pursued it with the sheriff."

"Well, we know it now. You said Sheriff Cheney is in an institution in Denver. Do you think he'd be able to talk with us?"

"I don't know."

"Well, I think it's worth finding out. How do you feel about a trip up to Denver?"

"When do you want to leave?"

THEY LEFT FOR DENVER THAT day in the buckboard, now dilapidated, that was given to Meelee by Charles ten years earlier.

Talkot trailed the wagon close enough to keep it in sight but far enough back to keep from being noticed.

The trip consumed the balance of the day, placing them in Denver at dusk. Meelee suggested seeking help from the Denver sheriff's office to locate the hospital that housed Darius Cheney.

Deputy Sheriff Phin Driskill, a tall, stocky man with a full gray beard and bushy, unruly hair, was as helpful as he was curious. He provided a sheet of paper with the name and location of the institution written on it and even gave them cursory directions to the location. "You come all the way from Bodeen to see him? Is he a relative or something?"

"I knew him when I was a boy," Foy said. "I was passing through Bodeen and I wanted to pay my respects, especially when I heard that he's so ill."

"Yeah, that's a shame. You might not be able to see him, though. If he's as bad as they say, he might not be allowed visitors."

"We have to try," Meelee said.

Driskill shrugged. "Suit yourselves."

They followed the deputy's directions and found the institution on a hilltop on the outskirts of Denver. The front desk required them to sign the visitors' log and then they were directed to Cheney's room.

A soft knock on the room door gained a husky call from within that granted entry. They were presented with a bed-ridden Darius Cheney clad in a hospital gown. The vast difference in his appearance between Meelee's recollection of him and this emaciated shell of a man obviously approaching death took Meelee by surprise.

"Mister Cheney," Foy said. "I'm Foy Banning, and this is Miss Amelia Scocroft. We'd like to speak with you if we could."

Cheney, beard overgrown and hair askew from contact with bedding, narrowed his gaze on Meelee.

"You look familiar, young lady." His voice was hoarse and weak. "Don't I know you?"

"Yes, we are acquainted," Meelee replied readily. "I knew you when you were the sheriff in Bodeen."

"Yeah, yeah," Cheney said. "I recollect you now."

Coughing interrupted Cheney from proceeding.

Foy, aware of the gravity of the man's condition, spoke when the spell subsided. "If this is a bad time, we can come back later."

Cheney waved his hand at them as he caught his breath. "Won't get no better waiting. This close to what's coming, I learned to do things now 'cause later might not be there. What's on your mind?" His words were interrupted several times by coughing and loss of breath. Through it, however, he showed a keen interest in the purpose of these visitors.

Foy moved closer. "Ten years ago, you investigated my father's death. Jeremy Banning was his name. He fell off a cliff. It was ruled an accident. But, when we went over your files at your old office in Bodeen, we noticed you made note of the fact that you were not convinced it was an accident. Can we talk to you further about that?"

Cheney looked off into space, appearing to be deep in thought. After a few seconds, he responded, laboring through further coughing spells. "I recall that. The fall broke him up real bad, but all the injuries were done to the front of the body 'cause of the way he landed. All 'cepting one, mind you. There was a small hole in the back of the skull, kind of like he was hit with something real hard back there. I thought it might mean something suspicious, but when I talked it over with the coroner, he said it weren't nothing. Could a happened any number of ways and none of them indicated anything criminal. He ruled it accidental, so I kind of had to go along with him."

"But it sounds as if you weren't really convinced," Foy said.

"Well, I was and I wasn't. The coroner was sure and it was his decision to make. But it always kind of bothered me. Just didn't sit right with me, but, then again, there really wasn't enough there to warrant a criminal investigation."

"That's exactly how I felt," Meelee said.

Cheney nodded. "You, too, huh?" Cheney endured another coughing spell and appeared quite exhausted when this one subsided.

"I'm sorry if we've overtaxed you," Foy said, "But I just had to hear this from you. Thank you for your help."

"Ain't nothing, son. So, what you going to do about it?"

A puzzled look crossed Foy's face. "I'm not sure. I certainly don't want to just walk away from it, not knowing what I know now."

Cheney loudly and angrily cleared his throat, obviously trying to prevent further interruption. "Let me tell you something. You get into this, it could be dangerous. If there was more to it, if somebody done something against the law, the party responsible could still be around. You start digging into it, you might just draw 'em out and they maybe come after you. And there's something else. Grael Renquist, your pappy's partner. You open this back up, he ain't going to be too happy about it. I recollect he was kind of in a hurry to get this buttoned up back then. He's got a big say in the goings-on in Bodeen. Swings a wide loop if you take my meaning. You do this, you could be leaving yourselves open to… well, let's just say, it might make Renquist a tad out of sorts."

Foy extended his hand to Cheney who shook it as vigorously as he could muster. "I do take your meaning, Mister Cheney. Thank you. We'll be careful."

"You better do more'n that. Better watch your asses."

8

TALKOT'S ALL NIGHT RIDE FROM Denver placed him back at the GR just before dawn. He was dog tired and ravenously hungry. Still, he knew better than to take time for those things when his mission to report to Renquist needed to be completed first. To that end, he dismounted in front of the main house and pounded on the front door. It took Renquist a few minutes before he opened the door and presented in a nightshirt, silk robe, and slippers. Rubbing sleepers from his eyes, he grunted.

"It's about damn time you checked in. What have you learned?"

"They must a got the key to the sheriff's office in town yesterday, 'cause they managed to get inside. They went through the files in there. Said something about some cuss name of Banning, Jeremy Banning, yeah, that's it. Talked about a accident that killed him. I couldn't hear it all, but that was a big part of it."

Talkot described Foy and Meelee getting into the old sheriff's office and spending some time there.

"From my guessing and from what I could hear, they just talked about some accident involving Banning's pa."

Renquist started pacing "That was yesterday. Where the hell were you all night?"

"I followed 'em up to Denver. Took me that long to get back."

Renquist began to show signs of tiring of this. "And what did they do in Denver?"

It was Talkot's turn to be frustrated. He let out a deep sigh. This was far from the ranching he signed up for, not for following a girl and tenderfoot to Denver and back. Talkot told Request about the pair visiting some old man at the sanatorium.

"I think it was Cheney. I reckon he used to be the sheriff here-abouts. I couldn't get close enough to the room, but the boy's pa came up. Your name was mentioned, as well."

"Then what happened?"

"They palavered some with him. I couldn't get close enough to the room to make out everything was said, but Banning's pa was mentioned. Heard Cheney say real plain to watch themselves, that you'd be pissed if they started poking around."

Renquist's interest piqued. "I see. Where are they now?"

"Reckon they're on the way back to Bodeen. Or they stayed the night. I don't know. Didn't wait around to find out. I hightailed it out of there 'fore they seen me. Figured you'd want to know."

"Yes, you did right. Get some food and some rest and get back to shadowing them. Stay with them. Tell me everything they do, everything you see."

Talkot turned to go back through the doorway, then stopped at the threshold. "What's this all about, boss? What's Banning's pa got to do with you? What the hell am I getting into here?"

"I don't pay you to ask questions. I pay you to do as you're told. Obey orders and stop being so curious. It's healthier that way."

Talkot's hand wiped at his mouth and tugged at his chin nervously. "Yeah, I reckon." He turned again and exited as Renquist shut the door behind him.

FOY AND MEELEE ARRIVED AT her home toward the end of the
next day. A modest white and green trimmed clap board cottage, the
house sat on a quarter acre just west of the cemetery. With a small
garden alongside it and a tiny one stall stable on the other side, the
house reflected Meelee's thorough and neat touch and her attention
to detail.

After unhitching and stabling the buckboard horse, Foy saddled
his rented horse and led it to the porch. Meelee waited for him near
the home's front entrance.

"Thanks for going with me," Foy said.

"I'm glad I went," she said. "You mentioned wanting to talk to the
coroner. What time are you planning to see him?"

"I guess about nine. That should give him time to open up."

"I'll meet you at the hotel before you go."

Foy took a step closer to her. "Meelee, you're going to lose too much
time from your work. You don't need to get any further into this."

"Yes, Foy, I do. I've waited too long already. The more we learn,
the more I'm convinced I should have done something about this
when it happened. I'm can't let it go now."

Foy reached to touch her arm, telling her silently he knew she was
dead serious. "All right, Meelee. But if this gets dangerous, promise
me you'll back off."

"I can't promise you that. I've got to see this through, no matter
what happens."

Foy breathed a sigh, reflecting his regret. "I should never have
gotten you involved in this."

Meelee placed a hand over his. "You did no such thing. I've always
been involved in it. I just didn't realize it until now. And, just to be

clear, I'm the one who brought it up. This is as important to me now as it is to you."

"I understand. I'll see you in the morning." Foy mounted.

"Good night, Foy."

His ride back to Bodeen and the hotel was pensive. Short of his visit to the coroner to request the exhumation of his father's body, he was uncertain how to proceed further with this. He also now bore the added burden of feeling responsible for Meelee's involvement, which could put her in danger.

How could he convince her to stay out of it now that she had become so adamant? Uncle Charles might have an answer to that, as well as what to do next, but turning to him for help would probably generate ill feelings about this mission. Charles would certainly advise against any further action and that would be diametrically opposed to Foy's intention to pursue this to its end. No, he needed to do this on his own and to protect Meelee in the process.

In his restless state that night, sleep was elusive. Foy spent several hours tossing and turning in the uncomfortable bed before he finally drifted off.

He experienced a vague happening that found him, a small boy riding Pony, following a rider that seemed to resemble his father. It was a fleeting image that went no further than the act of following this man. Then, abruptly, he awoke and looked around for something that was not there. A dream, he guessed. He passed it off as a manifestation of indigestion from an unpleasant meal. It warranted no further pursuit.

Rolling over in the bed, he tried to empty his mind and return to sleep. Eventually, after trying for longer than he thought it was worth, this worked.

In the morning, looking a bit haggard from his restless night, Foy met Meelee outside the hotel. They walked to the coroner's office without conversation. He thought about bringing up the dream but dismissed it as unimportant.

Reaching the office, Foy knocked.

After a few seconds, the knock was answered by a medium tall man with bushy, salt and pepper colored hair, copious eyebrows and a prominent nose. He had a full, mostly gray mustache and wore a white lab coat that bore blood stains that had not been removed by previous washings.

Foy and Meelee stood in the doorway.

"Doctor Janes?"

"Yes?" The doctor's voice was high-pitched and mousey, befitting his image.

"My name is Foy Banning. This is Miss Amelia Scocroft. We'd like to talk to you."

"How do you do. What can I do for you?"

"May we come in?" Foy asked.

Janes flashed a smile. "Of course." He stepped aside to admit them.

As they stepped inside, Janes removed the lab coat to reveal a slim, under-developed body and a curved spine that caused him to bend forward noticeably. He hung the coat on a hat tree in a corner of the room.

"Now, how can I help you?" Janes asked.

"Ten years ago, my father, Jeremy Banning, died in a fall from a cliff near the Sorrel Creek Dam. According to the inquest, you conducted the autopsy and ruled his death an accident. I've found reason to refute that finding. It leads me to suspect he was the victim of... well, let's say, *questionable* circumstances. I want his body exhumed so I can see for myself if it's true."

Janes was silent. He seemed engaged in studying Foy intensely.

His smile was suddenly gone, replaced by a look of concern. "What you ask is highly irregular." His voice was now agitated and at a higher pitch.

"I realize that, but I have to request it anyway. The questions this new information has raised can only be answered by an examination of the body. As his son, I feel I have that right."

"Mister Banning, this is not a question of right," Janes said, now taking an official tone. "It's a question of legality. For me to order an exhumation, I must have a legal reason to do so. Suspicion is not a legal reason. It is merely suspicion and nothing more. If I were to go around digging up bodies on the whims of suspicious relatives, half the graves in the cemetery would be opened. No, I will not allow that."

"I'm not asking for half the graves in the cemetery, Doctor, I'm just asking for one. And this is not a whim. I have it on good authority that there may have been foul play involved in my father's death. I'm asking for the chance to prove it or disprove it."

Foy read in Janes's facial expressions a resistance that he found to be excessive for the situation.

"And who would conduct this examination if I did allow this to go forward? Certainly not me. I have no reason to second guess my own ruling."

"I would."

"So, you're a trained medical examiner, are you?"

"No, but I feel competent to conduct this particular examination. And I know what I'm looking for."

"I'm very sorry, Mister Banning. I will not sign an exhumation order without hard evidence to support it. That is my final word on the subject."

Foy was prepared to carry the argument on, but Meelee interrupted, placing a hand on his arm as she spoke.

"Foy, it's obvious Doctor Janes is not going to cooperate. I think we should leave."

"But—"

"Please." Meelee cut him off with that single word, spoken very emphatically.

It was enough to stop Foy. Meelee obviously had a reason for her action. Frustrated, Foy nodded to her and allowed her to direct him toward the door. Nothing more was exchanged as they stepped out and closed the door behind them.

After walking a short distance, Foy halted, causing Meelee to stop also.

"Meelee, why did you do that?"

"Because he was trying to shut us down. And, if we continued, I was afraid we would reveal too much. I don't trust him, Foy, I never did. He always seemed cagey to me. And, after we spoke with Sheriff Cheney, I'm even more suspicious of him. Did you see his face? He knows more than he's saying."

Foy's face scrunched up in thought. He nodded. "You could be right. We'll have to find another way."

RENQUIST GLANCED OUT THE FRONT window of his house as the buggy carrying Dr. Janes arrived outside. The doctor pulled back on the reins to halt the horses and climbed out. After securing the lead strap to the hitch rail, he mounted the steps and knocked at the front door. Renquist opened the door and looked down at his visitor.

"What the hell are you doing here?" Renquist's question was brusque, bordering on anger.

"I had to see you. It's important." Janes was in an anxious state. He looked over his shoulder as if he'd been followed. Without waiting for an invitation, Janes pushed past Renquist and took a few steps inside. He immediately began pacing over a small area.

"Well?" Renquist said impatiently.

Janes recounted the visit from Foy.

"Why does he suspect his father was murdered? Come on, man, keep your head in this. Why does Banning suspect murder?"

Janes calmed a little. "He said he has reasons."

"And what are they?"

"I don't know. He didn't say."

"Of course not. And, of course, you did not press him. Precisely what did you tell him?"

"No. I told him no."

"Good. If he persists, keep refusing him, although I doubt he will."

"What do you mean? Look, Renquist, you can't get me any deeper into this. My nerves can't take it."

Renquist turned on him. "Shut up, you little pipsqueak! Your nerves were fine taking my money, were they not? Well, then, they will have to withstand seeing this through. Now, you get back to your office and stay the course. There will be no exhumation. Do you understand?"

"Y-yes. But what if he comes back?"

"I will see that young Mister Banning is handled. Now get out of here before you're recognized."

Janes hurried outside and, fumbling noticeably, got back into the buggy and drove away.

Renquist exited the house, walking quickly to the bunkhouse a short distance away. "Talkot!" His call came as he pushed through the door.

Asleep in his bunk, Talkot stirred and rose, resting on his elbows with his back off the bed, as Renquist approached. "Yeah, what?"

"Wake up!" Renquist shouted. "There's work to be done."

"Yeah? What's that?"

"Take three men. Find Foy Banning. Put the fear of God in him. I want him gone from here, straight away. I don't care what you have to do to make that happen."

"You sure you want to get the hands involved in this?"

"That's for me to decide. You tell them if they value their jobs, they'll do what they're told and ask no questions. Get them together and get moving. Banning was in town this morning. Find him. Deal with this."

Renquis watched as Talkot pulled his boots on, then picked up his hat and gun belt and headed for the door.

"Brent!" Renquist's call stopped Talkot. "Keep this quiet."

Without acknowledging the order, Talkot went through the doorway and hurried toward the stable.

IN MEELEE'S BUCKBOARD, WITH FOY'S horse tied behind, Foy and Meelee drove along the road from Bodeen to Meelee's home as the sun began its wan behind the mountains.

"Looks like we're at a dead end," Foy said. "I have no idea how to proceed. It's like we're blocked at every turn."

"We have to keep going. I can feel we're getting closer."

"I'm not stopping. But we need to think this through. I wish I was a better detective."

"I'm afraid we're both out of our depths here."

"Maybe we should talk to Mister Cheney again. This is more in his line of work."

"I agree."

As the wagon negotiated a bend in the road, four horsemen appeared on a hill a short distance away. Foy paid little heed to them. He did not question if Meelee had even seen them. The riders pulled up when they saw the buckboard.

The lead rider started out and the others followed. Their route was such that it would intersect with the path of the wagon. They increased their speed to a gallop.

As the horsemen pulled bandanas over their faces, Foy realized their intention was not friendly. Reacting quickly, he laid the reins across the rump of the horse and shouted at the animal to generate speed. Meelee seemed to realize then what was happening. She gripped the seat to keep from being thrown out by the pitching of the careening buckboard.

The sudden increased pace put the wagon in the lead as the masked men veered onto the road, now in a hard chase to run it down. Their stronger horses quickly shortened the distance, allowing Talkot to come alongside and overtake the buckboard. As he came neck and neck with the harness horse, he pulled his own animal sharply into it, causing a collision. This forced horse and wagon off the road. Already unsteady, the animal let out a frightened whinny as it faltered and fell over, pulling the buckboard over on its side.

Foy and Meelee were thrown from the wagon. They landed hard in the underbrush as the buckboard tipped farther, almost completely over, and then settled back on its side. The horse was able to regain its standing position while Foy's saddle horse was yanked until its reins broke free, allowing it to then scramble to safety.

Foy rolled with the fall and came to a stop several feet from the crash, He was stunned. Meelee hit the brush feet first, twisting an ankle and sustaining cuts and abrasions to her face and upper body. With the breath knocked out of her, she was unable to get to her feet, although still conscious.

The leader of the attackers waited until the dust began to settle.

Then, joined by his men, he rode to where Foy lay, stopping only feet away.

"Hey, Banning!"

Vaguely, Foy heard the call and directed what little attention he could muster to its source. The leader continued, "Pack up and get your ass out of here or you'll get worse than this."

Foy tried to shake some of the dizziness out of his head. He did not reply to the ultimatum. His head continued to spin and there was vague pain in several areas of his body.

"You hear me?" the man shouted.

"Yeah." Foy's reply was more of a grunt than a word.

"Your kind ain't wanted hereabouts. Get to moving out!" The leader pulled his horse around and led his men across the road and back up the hill.

Foy stared almost in disbelief as the intruders disappeared over the rise.

9

A FEW MOMENTS PASSED BEFORE Foy's head began clearing. At the same time, his tunnel vision began dissipating, allowing him to take in the scene before him. Aches and pain persisted from the twisting and the impacts his body had sustained in the fall. He pulled himself up on his elbows and was now able to see the buckboard laying over on its side. The horse was still hitched to it. The shortness of the lines pulled the animal to the point of falling, but it remained standing and struggled to break free of the harness. Across the road, Foy's horse stood grazing.

A glance to his right brought Meelee into his view. She was in a seated position on the ground with her legs stretched out in front of her. Hunched over, she massaged her ankle. Several cuts on the side of her face were visible. Immediately motivated to help her, he forced his legs under him and pulled himself to his feet. His legs were unsteady and everything hurt, but he pushed that aside and made his way, stumbling, to Meelee. He crouched beside her, seeing more injuries now. There were cuts and bruises to her face and upper body along with rips in her clothing caused by the rough brush into which she had fallen.

"Meelee, you're hurt." A second thought told him it was obvious and a stupid thing to say.

She looked up at him, pain apparent in her expression. "It's my ankle. I twisted it." Her voice was shaky.

Clinically, he pulled away her dress material to reveal the ankle. The top of her shoe reached above the ankle. Beyond that, swelling, forced higher on the leg by the confining shoe, was visible. He assessed the situation. Removing the shoe might make navigating on the foot more difficult. Most important at this point was transporting her to a place where he could administer aid and she could be made more comfortable. "I can't help you here." He spoke as much to himself as to her. "I've got to get you home."

He rose and moved to the wagon, already attempting to think through a way to get it back on its wheels. Satisfied with a cursory plan, he approached his horse carefully to keep from spooking the animal. His experience with Pony came into play as he spoke quietly and reached to take the reins that draped from the bit to the ground. He led the horse back toward the buckboard slowly. The animal reacted to the sight of the wreck by shying away. Foy slowed their approach. When he was sure the horse was comfortable, he reached the coil of rope from the saddle and looped it over the rear wheel hub. Then, mounting, he wrapped the rope around the saddlehorn and urged the horse away in a right angle to the buckboard. Straining, the horse pulled forward, forcing the wagon back over on all four wheels. It landed with a crash that could have caused any or all of the wheels to be crushed under its weight. He looked back to see that further damage was not incurred as the wagon rocked on its springs.

At the movement and sound of the landing, the harness horse whinnied and shuffled in the trace. Foy dismounted and went to the animal to quiet its fears. Several seconds of petting and soft speech settled the animal.

He removed the rope from the wheel and tossed it into the wagon bed. After examining the buckboard for soundness, he judged it still serviceable. He released the tailgate, then returned to Meelee and crouched beside her.

"Think you can stand?"

She appeared to be still somewhat lightheaded. "I'll try."

Foy went behind her and put his hands under her arms, lifting her. It was immediately obvious that the ankle was too painful for her to walk on as she faltered and took weight off it. He experienced pain from this action, but he pushed through it. Turning her, he scooped her up in his arms and carried her to the rear of the buckboard. Placing her in the bed of the wagon with her back against the side board, he secured the tailgate. He climbed up onto the seat and set the buckboard in motion, heading slowly back onto the roadway toward Meelee's home.

Upon arriving, Foy carried Meelee into the house and placed her lengthwise on the couch.

"Do you have bandages, medical supplies?" he asked.

"In the kitchen, bottom right cabinet."

"Don't move."

He hurried into the kitchen and searched for a few seconds before finding the cabinet she had described. There he located the supplies he needed. Along with bandages and clean cloths, he returned with a basin and a bottle of Burow's solution, an astringent liquid. This he used to clean Meelee's facial wounds as well as the cuts on her arms. When he was certain that these were properly tended, he turned his attention to her foot.

"I'm afraid this is going to hurt," he said as he lifted her foot.

She winced as he carefully removed the shoe. He gently examined the foot, noting the bruise and the growing swollen area around the ankle, now released by the lack of confinement. After wrapping it tightly from just above the ankle down across and under the arch, he brought her to a sitting position and crouched close to her feet. Placing her foot into a basin, he poured the solution over the bandage until it was saturated.

"That should reduce the swelling. You can use the solution many times. Keep wetting the bandage down." He stopped for a second as a different subject took over his thoughts and caused him to breathe a heavy sigh. "Damn it, Meelee, I'm so sorry this happened. You could have been injured much worse than this, maybe even killed."

"And so could you. Foy, this was not your fault."

"I can't help thinking it is. I should never have allowed you to get involved in this."

"We've been over this already. I was involved, I am involved, and I will be involved until this thing is settled." Meelee was resolute.

It was clear to Foy that pursuit of this would accomplish nothing. He changed the subject. "Those men that attacked us, I know they were masked, but did you recognize anything about them, anything at all? Could you have maybe seen them around somewhere, in town, maybe?"

"No, they didn't seem familiar at all. They could have been anyone. And I really didn't get a good look at any of them."

Foy pondered the attack. "They must be part of this. Nothing else makes sense. They weren't trying to rob us. They were trying to scare us off. Their leader made it clear they wanted us gone. Probably because we're getting too close."

"I agree."

"Does it frighten you that they've gone that far?"

"Yes, it does. But, more than that, it makes me angry and it makes me want to see this through even more."

"Yeah, I feel the same way, and I'm not backing off."

"What are you going to do?"

"I'm going to talk to that coroner again. One way or another, I'm going to force this out into the open." He got up and walked toward the door.

"Foy, please be careful."

"I will."

AFTER A HARD RIDE BACK to Bodeen, Foy pulled up hurriedly at the coroner's office and dismounted. As he stepped to the door, the door opened and he was confronted with Dr. Janes, whose exit path he blocked.

"What do you want back here?" Janes demanded.

The look of determination on Foy's face betrayed his intention before he voiced it. "You know what I want, Doctor. I want you to sign that exhumation order."

"Absolutely not! I'm completely satisfied with my findings in your father's case. It was an accident. As such it does not warrant exhumation. I will continue to refuse your demand, and if you don't stop harassing me, I'll have the law on you."

Foy glared at Janes. Uncertain if the threat was empty or not, he realized this was going nowhere. The doctor was in authority here and was determined to thwart the request. If Foy gave the reason for the request, he ran the risk of tipping his hand to whomever was manipulating Janes, indeed, perhaps the actual killer. Not wanting to take that chance, he decided to keep the information hidden. However, in doing so, he destroyed any chance of proving his theory. He was at an impasse.

"Now, kindly stand aside," Janes said. "Let me pass."

Foy hesitated for a second, then stepped back. Janes slammed the door and stormed past him, walking quickly up the street. Foy stood there, able only to watch the coroner walk away as frustrations rose within him.

LATER THE SAME DAY, RENQUIST poured over some papers at his desk in the study of the GR ranch house. A frantic knock on the front door pulled him from his work. He rose and strode to the door to find a distraught Dr. Janes standing there, wringing his hands and looking around fearfully.

"What is it this time?" Renquist asked, annoyed.

Janes brushed past Renquist and went inside. Renquist reluctantly closed the door and turned to address this disturbance.

"What do you want?" he said. "I'm busy."

Janes continued to wring his hands. He paced nervously. "It's Banning. He came back, still demanding the exhumation. My nerves can't take this. I'm beside myself. I can't make him stop. I even threatened to have the law on him. I don't think even that will deter him."

Renquist lost what little patience he had with this cry-baby, grabbing the doctor's coat and hauling him close. "You idiot! The law cannot be involved in this, even remotely. You know that."

Janes put his hand on Renquist's, trying to wrest himself free. He blubbered as Renquist pulled him closer. "All you have to do is continue refusing his demand. You have the authority on your side."

Janes forced his words out. "I can't do this. I'm afraid."

Renquist shoved Janes back, causing him to falter. Janes caught himself and managed to remain standing.

"You're afraid of Banning?" Renquist shouted. "No, you need to be afraid of me, not him. If this thing collapses, if I am put in jeopardy, I will make you very afraid, of dying."

"Please, you don't know. I can't—"

Renquist shook a finger at the doctor. "You can and you will. I have too much at stake here. You will see this through or you will be found on the side of the road, dead. Is that what you want?"

Janes cowered noticeably. "N-no."

"Then do what you have to. Now get out of here. I have no time for this."

Janes moved quickly to the door and exited. Renquist followed him and watched him climb into his buggy and frantically drive off. As soon as Janes was on his way, Renquist went on to the barn and saddled a horse. He mounted and headed quickly to the portion of the range at which Talkot and the hands worked. He hailed Talkot as he rode hard to join him.

"I told you to run that Banning kid off," Renquist said through clenched teeth.

"I did." Talkot seemed genuinely surprised.

"You did not. He was just in town, causing another disturbance."

"What do you want me to do, boss? He don't even carry a gun."

Renquist's anger came forth. "I do not care how you do it. Just deal with it. Do whatever you have to, but stop his incessant interference. Do you understand?"

"Yeah."

"Then get to it." Renquist turned his horse and rode away, leaving Talkot to gather his crew of raiders. Renquist stopped a short distance away and turned to watch Talkot assemble his men. He led them toward Bodeen. Renquist continued his journey home.

FOY RODE AT A SLOW pace away from Bodeen. Deep in thought, he racked his brain trying to formulate his next move in this cat-and-mouse game that threatened both his life and Meelee's. He failed to notice the four riders rapidly approaching him from the side until they were within striking distance. Recognizing the danger, Foy wheeled his horse and struck out at a hasty gallop in the opposite direction. But time was against him and, in less than a quarter mile, they had overtaken and surrounded him.

Talkot, riding parallel to Foy, reached out and grabbed Foy's jacket, effectively hauling him out of the saddle. Talkot's quick rein in dragged Foy across his horse's rump and dropped him heavily to the ground. The moving hooves of Talkot's horse narrowly missed striking Foy.

The attackers pulled to a stop as Talkot dismounted. He strode over quickly as Foy, dazed, tried to regain his feet. Talkot stepped in and delivered a roundhouse right that caught Foy on the point of the chin and ripped his head to the side. Momentum carried his body in that direction and he fell heavily to the ground.

Other men, now dismounted, stepped in, one delivering a kick to Foy's side as he tried again to get up. This drove him over onto his back. Another man kicked at him, catching him in the ribcage. Foy screamed and covered his face.

Now Talkot, down on one knee, straddled him and delivered blows to his face and upper body. Talkot straddled him, pinning his arms and delivering blows to Foy's face and ribs. The boy struggled to free himself and fight back, but found it difficult to breath and defend himself. Then he faltered under the barrage as everything went fuzzy and he felt himself slipping away.

The first shot shifted control of the situation. Foy saw through the haze that one of the attackers lost a hat to that bullet. Another whizzed past a second man as the report of the first discharge reached their ears. They looked out in unison toward the source of the shooting, a lone horseman riding hard toward them, his sidearm out and preparing to fire a third shot.

"Shit!" Talkot shouted. "Get out of here!"

His men scrambled to get to their horses and into their saddles before their horses took off down the road into the nearby wood.

The stranger kept coming. As his attackers disappeared into thick trees and underbrush, Foy watched helplessly as the rider directed his mount toward him. Dropping neatly from the saddle as the gray stallion pulled up sharply, he holstered his gun and hurried to Foy, going to a knee and removing his glove to examine the victim. Foy slipped in and out of consciousness as his perception became sketchy at best.

Medium tall and stocky, the stranger had a shock of curly black hair under his wide brimmed hat and was dressed in dusty, well-worn range clothes, including leather chaps. His face was strikingly handsome with boyish looks that combined with the weathering effects of long periods of outdoor life.

As he laid a hand on Foy's chest, Foy stirred and saw only a figure vaguely resembling one of his attackers. He attempted to defend himself by striking out.

The stranger grabbed the swung fist and held it.

"Hold it, kid." His voice was deep and husky, his speech slow and steady. "I ain't your enemy."

Foy sighed and fell back to the ground. Somehow, he couldn't figure out how, but somehow he felt he could trust this intruder. Foy's distorted facial expression betrayed the discomfort, but he was still far from fully alert. He did, however, manage a question. "Who... who are you?"

The stranger smiled. "Just call me Shawnee. What'd them waddies want of you?"

Foy winced and forced himself up on his elbows, though unsteadily. "Long story."

"I reckon. And you ain't in no shape for telling it now. We got to get you patched up." Shawnee leaned in to help the boy up, but Foy interrupted the process.

"Why'd you—"

Shawnee cut him off. "Four against one, friend. Them ain't the kind of odds I sit still for."

Foy's head reeled as he tried to pull himself up. "Thanks."

Shawnee nodded. He gripped Foy under the arms and hauled him up. Once Foy's legs were under him, he was able to help himself to a standing position, leaning on Shawnee for support.

"Let's get you back to my camp. You need tending to." He assisted Foy to his horse and up into the saddle. Then he retrieved the gray and climbed aboard. "Hang onto that saddlehorn."

Foy complied and, with Shawnee leading Foy's horse, they set out slowly into the countryside.

10

OY WAS YOUNG, MAYBE EIGHT years old, riding Pony, following that man who resembled his father. But this time, a little more of the experience was revealed. The man pulled up and dismounted at the base of a steep, rocky area. Foy kept hidden as the man led his horse up a rough path to join a figure who was shielded from Foy's view. As Foy crouched behind some bushes, the scene before him became cloudy and he found himself being whisked away into a haze. For several seconds, he floated there in nothingness. Then darkness replaced it.

Foy stirred and opened his eyes to find darkness all around him—the actual darkness of night. The last he remembered, he was being led on horseback by the stranger who rescued him. Back then it was still daylight. He must have passed out. He didn't remember getting off the horse or any of the activities that must have placed him in the current position he found himself, that of being on his back under a blanket. The last few moments, or what seemed like that, came to mind. That dream again, but this time, more of it. What did it mean? Was there any significance to it at all?

The pain in various spots on his face and on both sides of his rib cage superseded any consideration of the dream. He moved his hand to his upper body to attempt to identify the foreign substance that encased him and managed to identify it through touch as the shirt he had been wearing when the attack happened.

As his mind began to fully function, he guessed the garment was there as a binding to hold fractured or broken ribs in place. It felt tight as if it were tied in place. He remembered then having sustained kicks from both sides during the assault. The full incident then became quite vivid as images of the dream were relegated to the background.

"How're you doing?" a man's voice asked.

Foy looked in the direction of the sound, seeing at first the light from a blazing campfire, then a figure crouched close to it. His mind recalled the events leading up to the beating and the timely appearance of a stranger. He made the assumption that this was that man.

"I hurt," Foy said absently, "in a lot of places."

The figure rose and came closer, crouching as Foy pulled himself painfully onto an elbow.

"Reckon you would," the stranger said. "You just got the shit beat out of you."

Foy looked at the man, trying to put all the pieces of the occurrence together. He recalled the stranger giving a name, but it currently escaped him. "Sorry, I guess I was kind of out of it. What was your name again?"

"Names ain't important. Just call me Shawnee."

"Is that what your friends call you?" As soon as he asked it, Foy realized it was a dumb question.

The man shrugged. "Gray over there." He pointed to the gray horse grazing near Foy's horse. "He's about the only friend I got. He don't call me nothing, just tolerates me. Shawnee's good a name as any."

Foy nodded. "All right, Shawnee it is. I'm Foy."

"How do. Look, I cleaned up them cuts you got. Ain't sure about your ribs, though. Could be busted. I strapped them up all the same, but you ought not move about too much. Give them a chance to heal."

"Thanks. Tell me, why'd you get involved? You don't know me from a hole in the wall, and you had no idea what that was all about."

"What it was about ain't got nothing to do with it. Four against one ain't the kind of odds I cotton to. They just ain't—no matter who you be. Look, you need to rest just now. We'll talk more about it in the morning."

Shawnee was right. Exhaustion consumed Foy. He settled back on the blanket and allowed sleep to engulf him.

Early the next morning, as the sun rose, both occupants of the camp awoke at about the same time. Shawnee stretched and yawned while Foy winced as he found the several hours of immobility had caused more pain and stiffness from his wounds. He moved carefully to a sitting position, supporting himself on hands and arms extended to his rear. Feeling the morning chill, he realized his shirt had been otherwise utilized, leaving his shoulders and arms bare.

Shawnee pushed free of his bedroll and glanced across the dwindling fire to notice Foy's shiver. Moving around the fire, he picked up Foy's suit jacket which lay nearby and brought it to him. "Morning," he said as he draped the jacket across Foy's shoulders.

Foy felt the instant warmth of the fabric that had rested close to the fire and had picked up some of its heat. "Thanks." He pulled the garment close around him.

Shawnee placed more wood on the fire and stoked it to regenerate the blaze. "Let's get some food into you. Then I got to get you to a sawbones. I don't feel so good about them ribs of yours and I ain't fit to fix on 'em."

Foy felt around the area of his injured ribs as Shawnee pulled some jerky from his saddlebag.

"They don't feel broken," Foy said. "Definitely badly bruised. Fractured, maybe, but not broken."

Shawnee handed the food to Foy and took a bite of his own. They ate while they talked.

"How'd you know that, about your ribs?" Shawnee asked while chewing. "You some kind of doc?"

"I've seen enough of these injuries during games at school. You get to know by the feel."

"You ain't from these around parts, are you, kid? Now, mind you, generally, I don't horn in on other folks affairs, but I gotta say, you got me real curious."

"Shawnee, you were good enough to pull me out of a pickle back there. I don't mind you asking. I was born here, near Bodeen, but I've been away for a long time."

"What brought you back?"

"I'm on my way to medical school in California. I stopped off here to visit my father's grave."

"Sorry about your pa. Say, them *hombres* that jumped you yesterday, any notion what they wanted?"

"They were trying to scare me off. I've been looking into my father's death and it seems somebody wants me to stop."

"Why?"

Foy was hesitant to reveal more to this stranger, but something about the man invited him to continue. "I... I think there might be more to it, his death, I mean."

Shawnee seemed more interested. "More to it like somebody maybe helped him die?"

"That's what I'm thinking."

"And you think that's the hombre trying to run you off?"

"Yeah, I do."

"Well, that ain't at all very friendly. I might want to take a hand in that game."

"That might not be such a good idea. You saw how rough they play."

"I seen rougher'n that in my time. I just don't like the smell of this. But, you know, that's for later talking. Right now, let's get you some fixing."

"I don't want to go back to Bodeen. I don't think it's safe there."

"Know anybody hereabouts you can trust? You need to lay low and rest up some."

"There's the woman who raised me. She lives outside of town."

"Reckon we can go there if she'll have us."

"That shouldn't be a problem. I want to check on her anyway, make sure she's safe."

"All right then. You get done eating. I'll get us saddled up."

AFTER SHAWNEE'S COUNTERATTACK, TALKOT LED his men through thick underbrush and a densely-wooded area. When he was certain they were far enough away, he called a halt. They grouped around him.

"Get on back to the GR," he told them. "Back to what you was doing. Don't say nothing about this to nobody."

Quickly, they broke away from him and started out for the Renquist spread.

Talkot turned his horse and rode in the opposite direction. Carefully, he returned to the general area of the attack, staying hidden until he was sure there was no activity. He then directed his horse slowly into the center of the road to the point Banning had been thrown to the ground. Scrutinizing the area, he picked up the trail of two horses that led away from the area of the action. The tracks did not head for Bodeen which would have been the logical place to take a wounded man. They went off into the bushes and beyond into country unrelated to anything that happened here. Must have been that stranger taking Banning off to care for him. Certain Renquist would want to know more about this, Talkot followed the trail of hoof marks.

By nightfall, Talkot had tracked the two riders to their camp. This was evident from some distance by the yellowish, flickering light given off by the campfire. He stopped and dismounted far enough away to keep from being seen, securing his horse in some bushes. He crept closer on foot for a better look. Uncertain that the two men occupying the area were Banning and his rescuer, he took the chance of revealing himself by moving to within a dozen yards of the camp.

Positioning himself behind some bushes, he observed one of the individuals apparently tending to the other, specifically removing the shirt of the one who lay on the ground. Talkot watched as this man lifted the other slightly and wrapped the crumpled shirt around the other's mid body. After that, the man fetched a canteen and a cloth and gently cleaned the face of the other.

Now Talkot was convinced that these were the two he sought. Silently, he made his way back to his horse and secured his blanket from the saddle. Shrouding himself, he sat and waited. This would be another long night of no food and no sleep as he kept vigil. He would watch them until they moved and then would follow them wherever they went, no matter how long it took. Renquist would need to cough up plenty for this. He wrapped his arms around his legs and rested the side of his face on a knee, trying to find a modicum of comfort. That did nothing more than increase the distress this surveillance offered.

The first rays of the morning sun lit the range. Talkot came up with a start as the light and movement from the camp brought him out of a semi slumber. With enough daylight to now allow him to identify the two men, he watched the stranger move to the man who resembled Banning and hold a conversation with him. Shortly thereafter, the stranger kicked out the campfire and saddled both horses that were hobbled nearby. He assisted Banning onto his mount and, slowly, they moved out.

Talkot threw off the blanket and hastily rolled it and secured it to the saddle. Then he was up onto the already saddled horse and falling in to follow Banning and the stranger.

MEELEE SCOCROFT, SEATED ON THE couch in her parlor, lifted her foot from the basin into which the Burow's solution had drained after she saturated the ankle bandage. She had lost count of the amount of times she had done this exercise, but after several applications, she noticed that the swelling had decreased. As well, the pain and the sensation of heat in the ankle had dissipated. Foy knew what he was talking about. That brought her mind back to Foy and the fact that he had not returned the day before. She hoped he was all right and wondered about whether he was successful with his second attempt to persuade the coroner to order the exhumation.

Reaching down, she retrieved the bottle from which the solution came and inserted a large funnel into its neck. Then she carefully poured the solution from the pan into the bottle for reuse. By now, she had this process fairly perfected, spilling only a few drops. The towel spread out on the floor absorbed the overflow.

A movement from outside the front window caught her attention. Two horsemen rode slowly toward the house. One of them was Foy. She was certain of that, basing it on the clothes he wore. He seemed to waver in the saddle. Her attention was then drawn to his companion who was a complete stranger to her. The two moved across the field of vision the window provided. It looked like they were preparing to pull up at the front of the house.

Getting up carefully, she used the couch as a support, hobbling around the back of it and then advancing to other furniture for assistance in her approach to the door. She opened the door and leaned against the frame, taking weight off her wounded ankle.

Leading Foy's horse, Shawnee stopped out front. The cuts and bruises on Foy's face and the shirt strapped around his ribs were immediately visible to Meelee.

"Foy, what happened?" she asked. Surprise and distress registered in her voice.

"Four men jumped me on the road."

"Foy says we can stop here for caring, ma'am," Shawnee said. "That so?"

"Yes, of course. Come inside."

Shawnee dismounted and gently helped Foy out of the saddle. Meelee went back inside and made a place on the couch for Foy as Shawnee half-carried him inside. Meelee pointed to the couch and Shawnee deposited Foy there. He stepped back and removed his hat.

"Begging your pardon for the intrusion, ma'am, but we didn't have no other place to go. Foy didn't think it was safe for him in the town."

"It's all right. You're welcome here."

Foy looked up at Meelee, who was still standing behind the couch, using its back for support.

"Meelee, this is Shawnee. He drove off the men that beat me. Shawnee, this is Meelee… Amelia Scocroft. She helped raise me when I was a boy."

"Proud to make your acquaintance, ma'am."

"Likewise, and thank you, Mister Shawnee, for helping Foy."

"They ain't no mister to it, ma'am It's just Shawnee. You being a mite out of commission yourself, I'm obliged to do what needs doing."

"Thank you." Meelee sat down beside Foy.

Shawnee took command of the house. He strapped Foy's ribs with bandages Meelee had available. This freed up Foy's shirt so he could put it back on more properly. Shawnee fetched water from the well and chopped wood for the stove. After that he proved himself fully capable of accomplishing any task necessary, even to cooking up a tasty meal from Meelee's stores.

Meelee complimented his capabilities.

"Ain't nothing, ma'am. It's been just me and Gray—he's my horse— me and Gray for near ten year now. I want something done, I got to learn it or it don't get done."

Later, seated around the kitchen table, finishing their meal, Shawnee pressed Foy for more information. "What makes you think your pa was killed?"

"Something we found in the sheriff's notes. Because of the way he fell, there were no wounds on the back of my father's body except for one. The notes say there was a small hole in the back of his head. It was as if he'd been hit with something from behind. Nothing was ever made of it."

Shawnee leaned forward as Foy continued.

"The coroner ruled it an accident and the sheriff went along with that. We talked to the man who was the sheriff at the time. He still believes there was something more to it. So we asked the coroner to exhume the body—"

"Exhume? What's that mean?"

"They dig it up and examine it."

"Uh huh! So's the hole can be seen."

"Right, but the coroner refused. He said there was no legal reason for it. And, when we were on our way back from town, those same men that attacked me yesterday, jumped us and ordered us to leave."

"Who's the other part of the 'us' you're talking about?"

"Meelee."

"They put upon a woman?"

"Yes, that's how her ankle was injured."

"Son of a bitch!" Then, stopping abruptly at his choice of words, Shawnee turned to Meelee. "Begging your pardon for the language, ma'am, but that sure singes my hide. I ain't never made war on a woman and I'll abide no man that does. Ain't no question I be getting into this thing now. You tell me everything you know—*everything*. Then we'll cipher how we get to the bottom of this."

11

TALKOT'S SHADOWING OF THE TWO men went completely undetected by Foy and Shawnee. Keeping far enough behind to stay out of their view, he managed to keep them in constant sight. He counted on the fact that they were otherwise occupied and were not expecting to be followed. This worked for him.

He watched them combine their resources to find their way to the general location they sought. Once in the area, the wounded man made short work of locating the house. They approached openly.

Sure of their intention to seek help there, Talkot halted his mounted advance and elected to continue on foot. He secured his horse in some bushes and proceeded, keeping the two men in sight. He waited until they entered the building. Then he moved forward and selected a side window through which he hoped to gather more information. Since the window was shut, he was only able to observe their movements. Their speech was too muffled by the barrier for him to understand what was said. This was, however, enough to get him a good look at the stranger and to convince him that Banning had picked up an ally. After almost half an hour of peering in and making mental notes, Talkot withdrew and returned to his horse. He mounted and struck out fast for the GR.

His ride was swift and hard, bringing him to the Renquist's house by mid-morning. Tired and hungry to a fault, he knew his first mission was to report his findings to Renquist. Galloping into the area and pulling up short, he dropped quickly from the saddle and bounded onto the porch. The rapping on the door brought him face to face with Renquist as the door swung open.

"It's about time you showed up." Renquist sounded annoyed.

"I got plenty to tell you."

"Inside."

Talkot moved past Renquist as the older man closed the door. Talkot turned to face him.

"We jumped Banning yesterday like you said. We beat the living hell out of him."

"Good. That should make up his mind to get out."

"Well, maybe."

"What do you mean, maybe? I told you to make sure."

"There's more to it."

"Then tell it." Renquist reached the point of temper loss.

"Some stranger took a hand in it when we jumped Banning. Ran us off. Damn near plugged us all. When we got clear, I went back to the spot it happened at. Looked like the stranger picked Banning up and carted him away so I followed their tracks."

Renquist paced as Talkot continued.

"They spent the night in a camp up in the hills and me wrapped in a blanket watching 'em all night. Come morning, they packed up and headed over to that Scocroft woman's place. Couldn't hear nothing they said, but they sure seemed all friendly-like, the three of 'em, when I left to come here."

Renquist took in the information and pondered it. Talkot purposely did not interrupt this process. He knew better. After a few more seconds of pacing, Renquist turned to face Talkot. "I cannot afford to allow this to be made more public than it already is. We will wait to see what Banning does. Go back to shadowing him and report to me."

"One thing's sure. Banning's out of commission for a couple of days at least. He was having a hard time staying in the saddle on that ride to the woman's place."

"Excellent. He should have plenty of time to reconsider his actions."

"What about that stranger? Can't figure him out."

"A Good Samaritan at best. I'm not concerned with him, only with Banning. If the stranger presents a problem, he can be eliminated without drawing attention to me. Get yourself some food and rest. Then get back on Banning."

"Right."

DURING THE NEXT FEW DAYS, Foy and Meelee rested and healed while Shawnee completed whatever chores were necessary. Although they attempted to help, Foy and Meelee were told by Shawnee in no uncertain terms that their main jobs were to mend and that he was perfectly capable and content to do things himself.

Toward the end of the third day, Foy, over dinner, announced his intention to pursue the exhumation.

"You already told me the coroner ain't budging," Shawnee said. "You ask me, sounds like he's in somebody's pocket. Likely that same hombre that's trying to scare you off is pulling his strings to say no. How you plan to change his mind?"

"I plan to go over his head."

"How? Who's going to listen? I'd say the coroner carries more weight than you."

"I... I don't know. I'll have to... dig into that, I guess."

"No offense, but that don't sound like much of a workable plan."

"What would you do?"

"Me? I'd get me a pick and shovel and do the digging myself."

"But that's not legal."

"They ain't nothing about this is legal. You want answers, they'll come from working *out*side the law, like them owlhoots been doing."

At that point, Meelee interrupted. "Something's been bothering me, Shawnee. Why are you so interested in helping us? What's in this for you?"

"Nothing, 'cepting righting a wrong. I see a lot of me, my life, in Foy. Makes me feel kind of obliged to help him."

A confused expression crossed her face. "I don't understand. How are you and Foy similar?"

Shawnee leaned back in his chair.

"I was a young'un, year or two younger than Foy, I reckon. My pa got hung for riding with the Bushwhackers during the war. Reckon you heerd about Captain Quantrill and his raiders. Well, Quantrill suckered my pa into joining 'em. Sold him a bill of goods about taking back what the war took from the little folks. Soon as he found out the truth, he cut ties with them. But, by then, they'd already done some real bad things and him helping 'em. Folks found out about my pa. They tied Quantrill's reputation to him, so they took him out and strung him up. No trial or judge or nothing." Shawnee allowed the bitterness of the experience to show on his face and in his voice. "So, I went after them. Killed the leader of them Jayhawkers that hung my pa, but I wasn't particular careful about how I done it. The law come after me, and with no leg to stand on, I ran. Turned me into an outlaw with a price on my head, running to stay alive. They catch me, they'll hang me sure. I reckon if somebody'd a smacked me upside the head or something back then, instead of helping me get in deeper, things coulda been different now. I'm just trying to keep Foy from falling in the same trap."

"But you're asking him to go outside the law."

"No, ma'am, I ain't. I'm already outside the law. I'll do what he can't do. That-a-way, he don't break no laws." Shawnee turned to face Foy. "I'm going through my own brand a hell, brother. Ain't come out the other end yet. Likely never will. But you can."

"I can't ask you to put yourself in that position."

"You ain't asking, I'm telling. That's the difference. Let me take the chances. Anybody says anything about it ain't legal, the blame's on me, not you. And I'm gone like the wind 'fore they can turn around. I got real good at that. And maybe, just maybe, you'll find out what really happened to your pa."

Foy leaned back in his chair. "I don't know. I'm not sure about this. *Any* of it."

Shawnee rose and began clearing the table. "Deciding's yours. But you need to make that choice fast, reasons being them *hombres* are going to keep on coming at you till you're gone, one way or t'other. I ain't planning to be around these parts much longer, so I won't be around to help you. Too long in one place just ain't healthy for me."

Foy, deep in thought, said nothing.

"You ponder on it some," Shawnee said over his shoulder. "And you let me know."

Foy glanced at Meelee, then got up from the table and moved into the living room. Meelee followed. They spoke quietly, but Shawnee's keen ears picked up the conversation.

"What do you think?" Foy asked.

"I think we're at a dead end if we try to pursue this any further ourselves. No one in authority is going to take a chance ordering an exhumation on a hunch. Somebody, and I think I know who, is blocking us at every turn."

"Renquist."

"Yes. And remember what Sheriff Cheney said. Renquist is very powerful around here."

"I wonder if Cheney was pointing us in Renquist's direction without actually saying it."

"It's the only thing that makes sense, but we can't prove Renquist is involved any more than Cheney could."

"Not without examining Papa's body. I hate to admit it, but I think the only chance we've got is Shawnee."

"I think you're right."

The concern for involving Shawnee in this was present in both their voices.

Shawnee appeared in the kitchen doorway.

"Sorry for listening in, but I got pretty good at that, as well. You two going to kick this around all night or we going to get this done?"

Foy turned to him. "Are you sure about this?"

"About doing it? Yeah, I'm sure. Things I ain't sure of don't come out of my mouth. Now, first we got to make it look they done what they set out to do, like you caved and lit out."

"How do we do that?"

"You and me, we light out. We head for the hills and set up somewheres off the trail. Tonight. Miss Meelee, this is your place. You got a reason to be here so you should ought to stay. Go about your business. Just be sure you let it get knowed Foy left."

"Yes, I can do that."

"I'm ready to go when you are," Foy said.

"Good." Shawnee smiled and nodded. "Now, let's get some supplies together and head out. From here on, we do what we do after dark."

A few minutes later, after securing supply sacks to their saddles, Foy and Shawnee mounted. Shawnee had a final word for Meelee. "Anything happens and you need me, you'll find me at the cemetery tomorrow night, likely all night, I reckon. You take care now."

"Be careful," Meelee said as they rode away.

THE NEXT MORNING, TALKOT RETURNED to the area surrounding Meelee's home. Securing his horse in the same spot as he had used the previous day, he moved in and, taking care to stay hidden, took up his vigil at the same window.

The place was quiet. The only activity he observed inside the house was that of the woman. She looked to be going about her preparations to leave, maybe for work.

Talkot saw no sign of Banning or that stranger. Did they leave? Did Banning and the stranger maybe take the hint and clear out? He had to be sure. Renquist would not settle for a maybe. If the horses were gone and there were tracks indicating their exit, he would be more confident reporting that they had left.

He went around the rear of the house and moved carefully to the stable to find only one horse quartered there. Only one saddle was present. The only other tack he saw was directly related to the woman's buckboard which stood nearby. Studying the tracks outside the stable, he followed them to the front of the house. This told him Banning and the stranger had walked their horses to that point. Then they mounted and rode out. As he walked the tracks and studied the movement they indicated, Talkot's observation consumed his attention. This caused him to pay no heed to the fact that he stood out there in the open, his back to the house, in line with the front window.

A woman's voice spoke ominously from behind him. "Don't move, you! I've got a gun on you."

12

MEELEE WALKED TOWARD THE FRONT door. Making a final pass through the house to be sure everything was in order before leaving, she passed the window. She caught sight of a figure outside. Immediate recognition took place. He resembled one of the men who had attacked her and Foy on the road. Same clothes, same hat, same build.

She moved quickly to a small cabinet to the right of the kitchen doorway and pulled open the top drawer, revealing a Colt's 1860 Army model .44 caliber revolver inside. Lifting the weapon out of the drawer, Meelee went to the door and opened it quietly to keep from alerting the man. She raised the gun to line up with Talkot's back as she spoke. "Don't move, you! I've got a gun on you."

Talkot froze.

Meelee stepped cautiously off the porch, keeping him covered. Although she didn't cock it, the gun gave her more confidence, but she was not proficient at this sort of thing. She at least had to disarm him before she could safely question him. When she was close enough, she reached out with her left hand. Pulling the Peacemaker from its holster at arm's length, she tossed it aside.

As the piece hit the ground, Talkot spun quickly to his left, sweeping his hand to catch her revolver and shove it out of the way. His right hand followed with a clenched fist that connected with her chin and tore her head to the side, opening a cut at the point of impact. She fell backward and landed hard on the ground. The gun slipped from her hand in the process. Dizzy and semi-conscious, she lay still as Talkot stood over her. A few seconds passed as she tried to fight drifting away, but the battle was lost as she fell into a stark blackness.

ON THE GROUND IN THE same position for several hours, Meelee finally stirred and started coming back to consciousness, a slow process. Her eyes fluttered open to a clouded, upended view of scrub grass and dirt. Sense crept back into her being with even less speed, bringing with it the facial pain as well as aches throughout her body from both the contortion forced by the aftermath of the blow and by the prolonged irregular placement into which it dumped her. She groaned as she perceived the growing misery.

Blinking her eyes tended to make things clearer, but her position made the view distorted. For a few moments, until her brain began to process the scene before her, she lay still. As the events immediately prior started returning to her mind, she moved to right herself. This involved using an arm to hoist her upper body off the ground a bit so the arm on which she was lying could move. Having done that, she pushed herself to a position that allowed her to pull her legs under her. Pain increased in her head and from her chin. She became woozier. She held herself in the hands-and-knees posture for several seconds waiting for her head to clear enough to permit further movement.

When she felt more confident, she brought one foot forward and, putting her weight on that foot, pushed up. As she straightened, she became aware that her shoe was trapping her skirt to the ground. The push caused a rip in the delicate fabric of her petticoat and, as an extension, her dress. Unconcerned, she completed the move, ending up with major rips in the undergarment and the skirt.

Coming to an upright stance caused the dizziness to return. She reeled uncontrollably, spinning back to her hands and knees. Breathing a disappointed sigh, she shook her head to break free of the cobwebs and, with determination, tried again. Though this attempt was equally painful, she managed to achieve and then to maintain a standing position.

Orienting herself to her surroundings took some time. She glanced around to verify she was at home and that nothing but herself had been disturbed. The memory of the incident rushed in.

Instinctively, her hand went to her chin and felt the wound. It was still wet with blood although further exploration told her some of it had already dried. She calculated she must have been out for several hours. A look up at the place the sun now occupied in the sky confirmed that. It also brought back the whirling in her brain. She guessed she shouldn't have looked up or looked down or done either as quickly as she did. This forced her to reposition her feet to steady herself, bringing more pain, this from the ankle that had not yet completely healed.

Realizing she needed to find support, she inched toward the porch, contemplating taking a seat there. But as she drew nearer, it seemed too far and, even if she got to it and sat down, she might not be able to get up again from that far down. She reached the porch and grabbed the roof post. It took another minute of standing there and holding on before she was able to step up on the porch and shuffle to the door.

She opened the door and entered the parlor, making her way along the wall to the couch. There she sat, then placed her head forward toward her legs to help it clear. After a few moments, the whirling stopped and she slowly raised her head. Now her mind functioned closer to normal.

Leaning back, Meelee rested there for several minutes, mulling over what she had just gone through. And, from that, came a realization. She could identify her assailant. She got a look at his face. It was brief. It was fleeting, but she saw him just as he spun to hit her, saw enough to identify him. A wisp of a smile crossed her face at that thought only to be displaced by the pain it caused. Still she nodded slightly at this gain. She had him.

Returning to rational thinking, she tried to figure out what to do next. She needed to care for her injury. That would have to come first. Then a cleanup and change of clothes. She remembered Shawnee's instruction. If she needed him, he would be at the cemetery that night. It became her goal to seek him out.

Slowly and painfully, she moved into the kitchen and used water and a clean cloth to wash the blood from her wound. The cut still oozed a little so she continued dabbing it with the cloth. Afterward, she put pressure on it until finally the bleeding clotted enough to be left open to the air. She made her way into the bedroom and removed the dirty and ripped clothes. In their place, she put on the only riding outfit she owned, resolving to no longer encumber herself with restrictive clothing and the rigors and confines of the buckboard. From here on, she would ride the horse and dress for it.

AS THE WOMAN FELL IN a sprawl at his feet, Talkot rubbed his hands together, soothing the spots at which one had contacted her gun and the other struck her face. He studied her. She looked to be out of it enough that she would not be a further problem. His next thought was to get out of there quickly. He had been careless and now he was exposed. This made it necessary for him to get back to the GR where he'd be safer. He had to report this to Renquist anyway and to somehow set up an alibi in case the woman recognized him and took this to the law.

He stepped across Meelee's motionless body and kicked the revolver out of her reach, then retrieved his own gun and set out on a dead run toward the bushes where he'd left his horse.

Somewhat out of breath when he reached the animal, he glanced back at the house to be certain the woman was still down. Then he swung into the saddle and went to a full gallop to leave the area. Maintaining that speed over the entire distance back to the GR, he pulled to a hasty stop and dropped out of the saddle in front of the main house.

"Brent!" Renquist's call stopped Talkot and turned him sharply. Renquist strode out of the barn toward him.

"Got to see you," Talkot said shortly.

"In the house." Renquist pointed to the building as he joined him. They both stepped onto the porch.

Renquist opened the door to let them in and closed it quickly. He looked at Talkot. Renquist must have picked up on Talkot's mood from the look on his face because he voiced his observation. "You look as if you've seen a ghost."

Talkot hesitated.

"What the hell is wrong with you?" Renquist asked.

Talkot knew he had to tell it. How he did it would not matter. Renquist's reaction would be the same whatever words he used. "That woman, that Scocroft woman. I... I went back to her house to check on Banning like you told me. She was the only one around. It looked like Banning and that stranger lit out. So, to make sure, I checked the tracks in front of the house and—" Talkot stopped in mid-sentence.

Renquist lost what little patience he had. "Damn it, man, out with it." He was shouting now. "What happened?"

Reluctantly, Talkot continued. "She spotted me and pulled a gun on me."

"She saw you, saw your face?" Renquist was livid.

"Yeah… but I jumped her and slugged her. Then I got the hell out of there."

"Are you a complete idiot? Damn you! She saw you. She knows who you are, who you work for."

"No. Well—yeah, maybe."

"Maybe?" Renquist advanced on Talkot with clenched fists. *"Maybe? Without question, you goddamn fool. What the hell were you thinking? Were you even thinking at all? You left yourself wide open. And you've involved me."

"No, I didn't. I never said a word to her."

Renquist stomped back and forth, trying to control his temper. "Stupid! Stupid! You trespassed on her property and you assaulted her. She can identify you and make no mistake about it, she will identify you. That involves me, however remotely. Questions will be asked, leading to more questions, none of which I want asked."

"Well, what the hell was I supposed to do?"

Renquist flexed his hands open and closed several times but maintained reason. "You were supposed to stay hidden. What possessed you to show yourself?"

"I was trying to make sure they lit out. I knew you'd want proof."

"Not that way. Not right out in the open."

Talkot groped for an excuse. "Aw, I forgot she could a see me."

"You're an ass, Brent. And you let a woman get the drop on you.

And you left her alive to put us both in danger. At that point, you should have killed her."

Talkot felt his face go even paler. Wait, did he hear that right? "What'd you say? Kill her? Now, wait a minute here. I ain't no killer. I'll do a lot of things that ain't legal, but I ain't no killer. No, sir, I'm no killer."

"Well, now you have to be," Renquist said. "You have no choice."

"Oh, no! No killing!" Talkot fussed and grumbled unintelligibly for a second before voicing his decision. "You know what? I'm done with this whole shitting thing. I'm getting out. You pay me off right now! I'm getting out!"

Renquist stopped, taking a few seconds to work through this. Then he turned to face Talkot. "All right, Brent." He spoke in a calmer tone. "I'll pay you off. Perhaps it is best for you to go. Wait right there. I'll get your money."

Talkot stood by while Renquist went into the adjacent room, his study. Moments later, Renquist returned and handed a stack of cash over to Talkot.

"I think you'll find this more than covers what you're owed, Brent."

Talkot accepted it. He glanced admiringly at the wad but did not count it. It seemed like a fair sum. "Sure does, Mister Renquist. Thanks." He placed the money inside his shirt.

"You should leave now," Renquist told him. "Keep the horse and rig. You'll need them."

Nervously, Talkot said thanks a second time and moved to the door. He hesitated for a second, then he stepped outside, went straight to his horse and swung on.

"Goodbye, Brent," Renquist said from the doorway.

Talkot nodded and started out, heading west.

13

RENQUIST WATCHED TALKOT RIDE OFF for a few seconds. He stroked his chin and the wisp of a smile crossed his face. He nodded to himself, then hurried back inside to the gun rack next to the safe in the study. He selected a Whitworth .451 caliber long rifle and scooped up a case holding the items necessary to charge the muzzle-loaded weapon. With these in hand, he moved swiftly out and across the yard to the barn. In a few minutes, he exited riding the best horse he owned. With the tiny figure of Talkot in his view, Renquist also heading west.

He followed Talkot until they both were a good distance away from the GR property line. They were in hill country, covered with randomly placed rocks which made tracking somewhat more difficult. However, Renquist was an experienced hunter and, as such, he never let his quarry out of his sight. This was working out to be the perfect setup, the perfect cover-up.

Renquist stayed on Talkot until they were in an area that was almost completely clear of trees and bushes, a flat plain that afforded unobtrusive sight for a great distance. Halting, Renquist dismounted and assumed a kneeling position. He seated the Whitworth against his shoulder and braced his support arm on a knee for stability. The rifle came up, hammer cocked. The gun's graduated iron sights, upon adjustment, provided a perfect sight picture of Talkot's back. He sucked in a breath, let half of it out and pressed the trigger. The gun pushed straight back against his shoulder as the hammer struck and ignited the cap, blowing the powder and releasing the ball in a well-calculated arc. As the explosion resounded and echoed, the ball found its mark in Talkot's upper back. He pitched forward across the neck of his horse. His body went limp. Slowly, as the horse came to a stop, Talkot's body slipped to one side and was carried by gravity out of the saddle, thumping heavily on the ground.

Renquist, satisfied with the shot, relaxed from his position and got up. Without reloading, he slipped the rifle into its saddle scabbard and moved forward on foot. This accomplished his goal of leaving no signs of a second horse at the scene. Arriving at the body, he reached inside the shirt and withdrew the money, taking care not to disturb the position into which Talkot had fallen. Assured that everything was as he wanted it, Renquist returned to his horse and struck out in a different direction.

Riding hard until he reached the outskirts of Bodeen, he slowed his horse and entered the town behind buildings to keep from being seen. He directed his mount into an alley adjacent to the hotel and dismounted. Finding a protruding nail in the building wall, he secured the reins there and pulled the Whitworth out of its saddle holster. Carrying the rifle, he went to the back door of the hotel and tried it. It opened, allowing him entry.

How careless of them!

He moved inside with stealth and silence.

Knowing the layout of the hotel, Renquist crept to the staircase that led to the second floor. He peeked around it at the front desk. The clerk behind the counter dozed. The man's hands supported his face and he was far enough into sleep to be oblivious to any activity around him.

On tiptoes, he ascended the stairs. A creaking step toward the top caused him to stop. He waited a few seconds and, satisfied that nothing would come of it, he continued to the landing. Then a brief stop in the hallway to recall the room Talkot had reported was Banning's. Retrieving the memory, he quietly moved down the hallway to the door marked with the numeral seven. He leaned the rifle against the wall and produced a small pocket knife which he used to pick the simple lock. Once inside, he closed the door and lifted the mattress to almost shoulder height. He set the Whitworth between the mattress and the cross slats.

Being careful to replace the sheets, blanket and pillow properly, he exited the room and descended the stairs without disturbing the clerk. Quickly, he made his way out the back door and returned to his horse. He mounted and kept the horse to a walk until he was out of sight of the hotel. Then he broke into a gallop, confident that his plan, with the steps still to be executed, would not fail.

DRESSED IN A RIDING SKIRT, white blouse and boots, Meelee exited the bedroom, still favoring her injured ankle. She went to the cabinet from which she had obtained the revolver. From a different drawer, she pulled a holster which was slipped onto a smooth leather belt. She strapped it on and went outside.

In the diminishing light of dusk, it was difficult to see in the grass. She went to the spot on which she had fallen, indicated by the disturbed grass and dirt, and looked around. Locating the revolver, she picked it up and put it into the holster. It sat butt forward to conform to the holster's military design, but was exposed thanks to the protective flap having been sliced away. She was amazed at how much more confident having the security of the weapon made her feel.

Walking to the stable with a slight limp, she saddled the horse and mounted. Then, pushing through additional aches and soreness brought on by this new position, she set out for the road at a trot. When she reached the road, she urged the animal to a full gallop.

Darkness had fallen shortly before she arrived at the cemetery. She pulled up and scanned the area. There was no sign of Shawnee. Holding the reins, she let the animal graze close by. She waited. Somehow, although she hardly knew him, she was sure Shawnee would come.

After less than a half hour, a rider approached, riding slowly along the road. Meelee tucked herself and her horse behind a nearby tree, intending to stay out of sight until she knew the identity of the horseman. He stopped at the entrance and dismounted. The darkness did not allow her to make him out, but she was certain it was Shawnee. His wide brimmed hat and the outline of his chaps in the moonlight told her it was him.

She took a chance and called out to him. "Shawnee!"

He made a gesture of recognition and moved toward the sound of her voice. "Evening, ma'am," he said as he reached her. "Something must a happened to bring you here tonight."

"Yes."

"That the reason you're packing that iron?"

"Yes, but even with it, I feel safer being with you. I caught a man snooping around at the house today. I confronted him, but he knocked me down and got away. He was one of the men who chased Foy and me. But, this time, I got a look at him. I can identify him."

As she spoke, she turned her head slightly. The moonlight illuminated her face, revealing the cut on her chin.

"He do that to you?" He pointed to her wound.

"Yes."

"I'll remember that."

"I came to meet you because I didn't feel safe at home."

"Reckon you thought right. That hombre might could come back to finish whatever he had in mind. You come on back to camp with me tonight. You'll be better off there. Meantime, I got a job of work to do."

"I can help you."

"No, ma'am. What I told Foy counts for you, too. Don't want you—neither of you—going outside the law. That means no helping me. 'Sides, this ain't work for a woman. Truth be told, it ain't work for a man neither, but here we are. Look, you go ahead on back to the road. Wait there for me. I'll be along directly."

Meelee nodded, and Shawnee returned to Gray. He picked up the reins and led the horse into the cemetery.

AT THE GRAVESITE A FEW minutes later, Shawnee untied a sack of tools from behind his saddle. He pulled out a pick and shovel and dropped them at his feet. The last item he took out was a coal oil lantern. He lit it and set it beside the grave. For a brief moment, he dwelled on the fact that Meelee had told him twice in so many minutes that she felt safer around him. Truth be told, he did admire being in her company, as well. Then, dismissing the thought, he went to work.

After an hour of digging, Shawnee took comfort in the fact that it was a shallow grave. The plain pine coffin became available after the removal of only a couple feet of earth. As he cleared dirt from the top and one side of the box to allow himself access, he already began to detect the smell of the decomposed corpse within. He stopped and pulled his bandana over his nose to help shield out that which promised to become overwhelming. Steeling himself, he finished what was likely the most undesirable work he'd ever done. Using the shovel blade to lift the cover of the box, he pried it back. It made squawking sounds as rusted nails were pulled from their decade old seats. The odor released by the opening caused him to pull back. It almost overpowered him. Finding the bandana to be only a minor assist, he was forced to turn away to catch his breath. He coughed for several seconds, trying to suck in fresher air to displace the pollutant.

Bringing the lantern closer, Shawnee braced himself for the unknown as he slowly swept his gaze into the coffin. It was hideous. Discolored skin had turned leathery and had dropped away from the bones. That had revealed many breaks in those bones. In the midst of it, maggots squirmed and fed vociferously. Moisture, having crept in over time from the surrounding soil, collected in several pools around the body, adding to the stench. He had to work fast because prolonged exposure to this odor would likely overcome him. Reaching in, he gripped the skull with his gloved hand. Folds of decayed skin hung from it. There were multiple cracks and fissures on the front, likely caused by the impact of the body's landing.

Balancing the base of the lantern on the corner of the coffin, he turned the cranium to view the back of it, wiping away foul wetness and debris that had collected at the floor of the casket. Here there was no damage at all, save for a small break at the base no more than an inch in size. No way that was done by the fall. No way in hell. He made a mental note of the size and location and quickly replaced the skull back in its approximate position in the coffin.

Shawnee leaned away again to inhale several deep breaths of fresher air as the odor almost overwhelmed him. A little more of that stuff and he would have passed out. He set aside the lantern and pulled the cover down hard, then he used the shovel to reseat the nails. Scrambling out of the hole, he took several seconds to clear his lungs and his head before beginning to shovel the earth back in.

The entire operation consumed several hours. At about two in the morning, Shawnee, exhausted, emerged from the cemetery to find Meelee patiently waiting at the side of the road. She leaned against a tree and fiddled with her horse's reins.

"I can't imagine what that must have been like," Meelee said as he walked Gray closer.

The odor that had attached itself to Shawnee's clothes, combining with the filth and encrusted sweat, repelled her. She backed up a bit, uttering an unintelligible sound of disgust.

Shawnee stopped where he was. "Sorry. Couldn't help it. I don't never want to do nothing like that again. Needed doing, though. Foy was right. His pa got whacked a good one backside of the head."

"I knew it."

Meelee showed both elation and sadness at the news.

Shawnee stepped into the saddle. "Let's get out of here," he said flatly. "Stay a few feet back of me. I surely do stink."

Meelee chuckled as she mounted and fell in behind Shawnee. Slowly, they rode away.

14

THE CAMPSITE SHAWNEE HAD CHOSEN was in hilly terrain high up at the top of a rough path that wound through rocks and boulders. At several points, single file passage was required and, at one point, horses with riders could not pass. Each horse had to be led carefully through by its dismounted rider to prevent cuts and scrapes from jagged protrusions.

Alone in the camp, Foy felt secure enough in his location that he finally relaxed and acknowledged the need for sleep to replenish him. It was about midnight when he lay down close to the fire. He allowed the dancing flames to mesmerize him. Shortly after, he succumbed to slumber.

It was nothingness at first. Then slowly he became aware of a cloudy existence in which he was again that eight-year-old boy who had followed his father on that morning. He saw himself kneeling behind that bush and looking up as his father climbed the path that led to the cliff. But this time, the entire incident played out in front of him. And he recognized the man his father met up there. It was the neighbor, Mr. Renquist. There was an initial discussion between the two men. As they talked, they moved together to the edge of the cliff. Then Mr. Renquist took a step back and got something from his horse. He swung it at Papa. It hit him in the back of the head and Papa fell, disappearing from sight.

Young Foy could not see where his father landed because of the rock face that intruded into his view. Horrified, he was transfixed, frozen in place. He now realized, within the dream, that he had witnessed his father being murdered by Mr. Renquist. But, back then, it was too much for his young mind to comprehend or to process, so he made believe it did not happen.

He was still there, hiding in the bushes, when Mr. Renquist came down the path and found him.

"Foy Banning," Mr. Renquist said. "Is that you?"

At that point, dumbfounded and wanting to cry out his accusation to the assailant, the scared little boy simply and hesitantly answered, "Yes, sir."

And, in a second, at the full sight, up close, of his father's killer, the incident was gone, erased from his memory. He allowed Mr. Renquist to take him in tow.

"Foy! Foy, wake up!"

It was Meelee's voice and it was pulling him from this horrific scene, this dream that had finally shown him the whole incident and brought his mind to a point of complete comprehension. He bolted breathlessly to a sitting position, to see Meelee bending over him. Past her shoulder, Shawnee stood with the horses.

"What—?"

"You were dreaming. You were calling out, 'Papa, Papa!'"

Then everything was clear, crystal clear, to him. "Meelee, I know who killed Papa. It was Renquist. I was *there*. I saw him do it. He hit Papa in the back of the head and knocked him over the cliff. I saw it! I don't know why I couldn't remember it then, but I know he did it. I saw him do it."

"It must have been too painful for you to remember. You were only eight, and you'd just seen your father killed right in front of you. I don't think I'd want to remember that either, at any age."

Shawnee extended a hand and helped Foy up. "Falls in with what I found at the grave. Leaving out the gory parts, your pa's skull shows that wound you seen in the dream. Wouldn't be surprised if it killed him before he hit the ground."

"Thanks for that. I'm not sure I could have gone through with it."

"Truth be told, I weren't sure myself, but it's done. Now we know for sure who we're after, we can make some plans. Meelee had a run in with one of them waddies that chased you t'other day. She can point him out." Shawnee placed his clenched fist against his open hand to illustrate his meaning of his statement. "We get him, maybe we can convince him to rat out Renquist."

Foy finally turned with concern to Meelee over her encounter with Talkot, finally seeing her facial wound. "He hurt you."

"I'm all right, Foy. It was worth it to be able to identify him."

"Time to clean up and bed down," Shawnee said. "Come morning, we got us some ciphering to do."

"BRENT IS MISSING." RENQUIST ADDRESSED six of his hands from the ranch house porch. They had gathered at his call and now reacted with concern at his announcement. "The last I saw of him was two, almost three, days ago. He said he had picked up the trail of some rustlers. He was heading west. He said he would come back for us when he located them. I believe he might be in trouble. Get your horses. We're going out to find him."

He had waited an appropriate amount of time to spring this.

There had to be a long enough interval to make the disappearance believable. His guess at two to three days appeared to be sufficient since the hands responded as if they bought it. His attempt at sounding distressed also seemed to have worked.

The hands headed for the barn to secure their horses. Within ten minutes, they were mounted and grouped outside the barn. Renquist led his own horse out of the barn, mounted and led them out. They headed west.

Without being blunt about it, Renquist maneuvered the search in the general direction of the spot at which Talkot had fallen. He followed a seemingly erratic pattern that perpetuated the ruse that finding the body would be by random chance. As they approached the area of the killing, he offered a direction, pointing to a flatter region that had less rocky obstructions. "There's nothing here. Let's try over there."

The group moved into that section. Renquist allowed one of the hands to make the discovery.

"Hey, I see something." The man pointed to the spot that attracted his attention. "There."

Every eye followed the man's finger and each saw the outline of what appeared to be a body about two hundred fifty yards away. A saddle horse grazed several yards from it. At once, they were in motion, riding hard toward the spot.

They pulled up hard about fifty feet from what was now clearly a body. Renquist dismounted and approached while the cowboys remained mounted. Performing the obligatory examination for signs of life, Renquist rose and faced the group. "It's Brent. He's dead. Shot in the back." His words were carefully chosen to further incite anger in the group.

Discussion among the hands followed as Renquist returned to them. He singled out a thin, wiry built man with a long face and a tall crowned hat. "Locke, go back to the GR and get a fresh horse. Then ride like hell up to Denver. Tell the sheriff about this. There is a killer on the loose. Go fast. We'll wait for you in town."

Locke pulled his horse around sharply and set out in the direction of the GR at a gallop.

"Get Brent up on his horse," Renquist told the others. "We'll take him into Bodeen."

Quietly, they carried out the order as Renquist stifled a smile, satisfied with the way this was working out.

———————

THE NEXT DAY, DEPUTY SHERIFF Phin Driskill, riding beside Locke, entered Bodeen. As they approached the jail, Renquist stepped from the coroner's office. He entered the street to intersect their path and waited there for them to reach him. The two riders drew rein a few feet away from Renquist.

"Mister Renquist," Driskill said in greeting.

"Deputy," Renquist offered his hand as the lawman climbed down out of the saddle. "I assume that Locke here has told you what has happened to my man?"

"That's why I'm here. I'll need to see the body."

"Of course. He's at the coroner's office."

The deputy directed his horse to the hitch rail outside the coroner's office. He dismounted and entered the building. As the door closed, Dr. Janes entered from the operating room.

"Good day, Deputy. I assume you're here about the body Mister Renquist brought in. I was just about to start the autopsy."

"Let me see the body before you start. Then I'll wait for the report."

Driskill's examination of the body took only a few moments. He verified the location of the single gunshot wound in the victim's back. "Looks like he never seen it coming."

During the several hours that followed, the doctor conducted the autopsy alone in the operation room while Driskill waited in the outer office. When Janes finished, he emerged, drying his hands in a towel. He sat down at his desk and wrote out the report which he then handed to Driskill.

Driskill scanned the document before leaving in case he had questions. Coming up with none, he left the office to walk to the saloon. As he entered the establishment, several citizens crowded around him to request information. Renquist pushed his way through these people to face the deputy.

"What have you learned?"

"The doc dug a four-fifty-one ball out of Talkot's back. There's only one gun I know fires a round that size—a Whitworth rifle, the one they used in the war. Know anybody that carries one?"

Renquist feigned pondering for a few seconds. "I do actually. There is a young man, a stranger here. He has one. I've seen him carry it."

The group around them engaged in discussion about this.

"What's this gent's name and where can I find him?" Driskill had to raise his voice to be heard over the group's noise. "Hey, shut up, will you? I can't hear myself think."

The crowd quieted down enough for the conversation to continue.

"His name is Banning. Foy Banning," Renquist said. "He arrived a few days ago. I'm not sure where he is now, but I do recall that he and Brent had words at one point. I could not hear what it was about, but it almost came to blows. Thankfully, Brent backed off."

The surrounding discussion increased in intensity.

"Keep it *down*, I said!" Driskill shouted. Then, to Renquist, he stated, "I'll need to talk to this Banning *hombre*."

"I believe he's staying at the hotel. He has also been seen in the company of a woman, Amelia Scocroft. She lives west of town off the main road."

"Thanks, I'll check it out."

"It's the least I can do for Brent. He was a good man. His killer should be brought to some swift justice."

The crowd became more incensed by these words.

"He will if I have anything to do with it," Driskill said.

The group began making references to taking the law into their own hands—some louder than others.

Renquist intervened. "Please, gentlemen, we must let the deputy do his work. We must follow the law."

"Mister Renquist's right," Driskill said. "I got enough to do without keeping eyes on you folks." He shook his head and left the saloon.

The hotel clerk was about to nod off when the deputy's noisy entrance abruptly shocked him back to reality. "How do, Sheriff."

"Deputy," Driskill said as he stopped at the desk.

The clerk seemed uninterested. "Oh, right, right."

Driskill got right to the point. "What room is Foy Banning in?"

"Why, number seven, but he ain't there now." The clerk looked like he wanted to doze again.

"Don't matter. Give me the key."

"But it's—"

Driskill was having no refusal. "This is official business. Now you give me that key or I'll run you in for obstruction."

"For what?" The clerk looked puzzled.

"Never mind! Just give me the goddamn key!"

The loud words motivated the man. He reached behind him to the rack and handed number seven's key over.

"You can go back to sleep now," Driskill said as he turned away.

He mounted the steps in twos and went quickly to the room. Unlocking the door, he entered and went directly to the chest of drawers. Finding nothing of interest in the bureau, he looked around at the rest of the room. Nothing else was there save for the bed. He'd seen that done before. He lifted the mattress, revealing the rifle. After picking up the weapon, he dropped the mattress and examined the piece. The manufacturer's markings on the barrel identified it as a Whitworth. Glancing at the mattress, Driskill noticed that it had fallen in a haphazard manner. He gave this no concern. He'd have the man in custody before he became aware of the unauthorized entry. After a quick last look around, he left the room without locking the door.

The sound of the key dropping on the counter snapped the clerk out of another nap attempt. Driskill walked to the front door and stepped out as the clerk picked up the key and returned it to its berth.

Driskill returned to the saloon and approached the waiting Renquist who was seated at a table with a drink in front of him.

"I see you found the gun," Renquist said.

"Yeah, but no sign of the owner."

"He may be with that woman."

"Yeah, that's why I come back. Where'd you say she lives?"

"Take the west road out of town for about a mile. It is a white and green house off the north side of the road."

––––––––

THAT SAME MORNING, SHAWNEE SAT with Foy and Meelee around their campfire. Having found a stream nearby, he was able to wash away the grime of the dig and the stench of the decomposed body before turning in the night before and was now dressed in the only change of clothes he owned.

"We should take what we've learned to the authorities," Foy said.

"What are you going to tell them?" Shawnee asked. "That we dug up a grave we had no right putting a shovel to? 'Fraid that ain't going to stand up in a court or anywheres else. We got to handle this our own selves or it ain't getting done."

"But how? Renquist seems to have all the power here."

"We use his power against him, make it so tough for him he makes mistakes, mistakes that'll trip him up."

"Looks like you've got more ideas about this than I have."

"Only way I survive is to think on my feet. And I ain't bound by no rules like you. For me, it's whatever works and don't get me killed. I ain't worked it all out yet, but I will. Till I do, we'll hide out here."

"Then we'll need more supplies," Meelee said. "I've got plenty at my place. We won't need to go anywhere near Bodeen."

"All right. Reckon you and Foy can handle that. While you're gone, I'll take the Yellow Boy out and see if I can bring down a deer."

"What if they find the grave disturbed?" Foy said.

"Truth be told, I hope they do." Shawnee flashed a grin. "Maybe that'll shake Renquist up enough to make him miss a step."

Within a few minutes, Shawnee pulled his Winchester from its saddle holster and disappeared into the tree line above the camp.

Foy and Meelee mounted and started for her home. Their ride was uneventful until they came within sight of the house. Coming off the main road, Foy pulled up abruptly, causing Meelee to rein in beside him.

"You've got company," he said.

She looked to where Foy pointed. A lone saddle horse stood outside the house. "Never saw that horse before," she said. "I want to know who it belongs to. Wait here."

Before Foy was able to react, Meelee urged her mount ahead. At a fast trot, she rode to the house and dismounted alongside the unfamiliar horse. Stepping onto the porch, she drew her sidearm and held it muzzle up at shoulder level. Her entry through the already open door was swift. Settling her gaze on the figure inside, she brought the gun to level, covering him.

Driskill, searching the cabinet beside the kitchen doorway, turned at the noise of her entry.

"Don't move!" Meelee said.

It was then that she saw the badge on his vest. He placed his hands out palms down. "Whoa, now, missy. I'm the law. You're the one best not moving."

Meelee held her position. "I don't care who you are. What are you doing in my house?"

"I'm here on official business. Looking for a fellow name of Banning. I'm told you been seen in his company of late. You'd best tell me his whereabouts."

"Why are you looking for him?"

"I want him for questioning in a murder."

"What murder?"

"Lady, you need to be answering my questions, not asking your own. Now put up that gun and talk to me."

Meelee weighed the alternatives available to her, continue to hold a deputy sheriff at gunpoint and risk further consequences or cooperate and get him to leave peacefully. She chose the latter. Without a word, she holstered her weapon.

"I'll just hold on to this awhile." He stepped close to her and lifted the gun out of the holster. "Safer that way. Now, where's Banning?"

"I have no idea."

"How do you explain being seen with him?"

"I knew him when he was a boy. We were just catching up."

Driskill studied her for a second. "Somehow, I don't buy that. There's more going on 'tween you two than you're letting on. I'd bet on that. Maybe a little time behind bars'll loosen your tongue."

"You're arresting *me?*" Meelee was genuinely astounded by the deputy's words.

"Yup. Complicity in a murder, less'n you want to give Banning up."

Meelee decided to stonewall the deputy. "I told you I have no idea where he is."

Driskill shoved the revolver into his waistband. "Well, then, we'll be heading you to jail."

At that, Foy stepped fully into the doorway. "Leave her alone! I'm the one you want. I'm Banning."

Driskill drew his own handgun and pointed it at Foy.

"Foy, no!" Meelee said sharply as she turned to face him.

"I want to see them hands up, Banning," Driskill said. "You're under arrest."

"On what charge?"

"Suspicion of murder."

"What? Who the hell am I supposed to have murdered?"

"Brent Talkot."

"That's crazy. I don't even know anyone named Talkot."

"Never mind that. Just get 'em up. Time for talk when you're in a cell."

Foy raised his hands to shoulder level.

Driskill stepped past Meelee, pulling handcuffs from the back of his gun belt. Pushing Foy around to face the doorway, he pulled each hand behind him and locked a cuff around each wrist. "Where's your horse?"

Foy sighed and jerked his head out past the fence. "In those trees over there."

"All right, get to walking. Just remember, one wrong move and I'm within my rights to put you down. And I got no problem doing that."

Foy started walking toward his horse. Driskill mounted and turned to follow Foy. Meelee stepped out onto the porch. "Hey, what about my gun?"

"I'll just keep it in custody a spell so's you don't get yourself in more trouble," Driskill said over his shoulder. "Just be thankful I ain't running you in with him."

Meelee issued a grunt that betrayed her anger and frustration. She watched as Foy reached his horse and stopped, unable to mount without the use of his hands. Driskill got down and assisted Foy into the saddle and then remounted and took Foy's reins in hand. Leading Foy's horse, he turned to ride toward the main road. When they were well on their way toward Bodeen, Meelee mounted and broke out at a gallop, heading back to camp.

15

BEARING THE WEIGHT OF A freshly killed mule deer across his shoulders while he carried his Winchester, Shawnee walked slowly into the camp. His eyes scanned the area carefully, but he saw nothing out of the ordinary. The fire still burned, but it had waned during his time away. It would need more wood to keep it going. That could be done later.

Satisfied that everything else was intact and undisturbed, he walked over to the boulder which provided a back wall to the camp and let the carcass slip from his back to the ground. He propped the rifle against the boulder.

The kill needed to be butchered and cooked before it spoiled or the whole process would have been a waste. It was bad enough that a good part of the animal would be scrapped because he lacked the means to preserve it or to smoke it. Not to save the portion he could save would be just wrong. Ignoring the tiredness in his body, he found his skinning knife in his saddlebag.

As he made the first cut, Shawnee's attention was drawn to the camp entrance by the sound of a rider entering. He looked around to see Meelee ride in quickly and dismount.

"Shawnee!"

The ominous tone of her voice and her concerned expression told him she did not bring good news. He rose and started toward her, leaving the knife imbedded in the meat. "What's wrong?"

"Foy's been arrested."

"What're they charging him with?"

"Murder. They say he killed Brent Talkot. I think he was Renquist's foreman."

Shawnee raised a hand in a halting gesture. "Hold on a mite there. Foy ain't no killer. He ain't even had the chance."

"I know. But the deputy who was at the house thought he is. He was looking for Foy. He threatened to arrest me to make me tell him where Foy was. That's when Foy surrendered to him."

"To save you, I reckon."

"Yes."

Shawnee nodded. "I'd have did the same, it was me. Where they at now?"

"On their way to town."

Shawnee paced a few steps, deep in thought, then turned to her. "Ain't saying it's the best place for him, but sitting in a cell ain't the worst, neither. At least, he can't get into more trouble. I reckon now we got to speed things up."

"How do we do that?"

"That coroner, what kind of *hombre* is he? He scare easy?"

"I think so. He's kind of mousey. He seemed very nervous when Foy and I talked to him."

"Good. That'll help. Reckon I'll pay him a little visit. Time to shake things up a mite." As he spoke, Meelee chewed on her bottom lip, making him aware of her preoccupation with something. "Problem?"

"It's my fault Foy was arrested. If I didn't bring up the supplies, we'd both still be here and he'd still be free."

Shawnee placed his hands on her shoulders in a gesture of caring and support. "You can't be doing that to yourself."

"But I got him into this. I'm the one who first brought up the notion that his father might have been murdered. If I'd have kept quiet, he would have just visited his father's grave the way he planned and then left Bodeen."

"Now, you stop that. You just put that right out of your head. Ain't none of this on you. He'd have recollected what he seen as a kid sooner or later. By then, maybe we ain't around to help him. Maybe he bulls into it on his lonesome and gets his self killed."

She appeared to consider that for a second. "I guess you're right."

"'Course I'm right. You got to quit beating on yourself."

She smiled sheepishly.

Shawnee stopped talking. He stared at her as he realized he had called her by her given name and he had touched her as if they were close. He told himself it was only to settle her down, but he had to keep that in check. He definitely felt something for her, but getting involved with her would never work out. He knew that. Releasing her arms, he turned away.

Meelee seemed to pick up on his uneasiness, his awkwardness. "Shawnee, what is it?"

"Ain't nothing," he said, still facing away from her. "It's just.... Forget it. Ain't nothing."

He returned to the deer carcass and resumed the butchering operation, leaving Meelee to stand there, a puzzled expression on her face.

When the cuts were ready and laid out on a blanket, Shawnee built a makeshift spit out of stout branches and started a separate fire, larger than the campfire. He inserted the meat onto a sharpened branch and set it over the fire, at a height that allowed cooking without burning the wood. He showed Meelee how to rotate the meat for even cooking and then cleaned himself up and prepared to leave camp. Before going, he picked up the rifle from its prop against the boulder and handed it to Meelee. "Know how to use this?"

She took the weapon. "Yes, I do."

"Keep it close. See you stay here in camp. Don't want nothing more happening to you."

"I will."

Shawnee noted how aloof Meelee had become since their conversation earlier. As strained as it made him feel, he judged it a good thing. Better to keep space between them than to become further involved. That would just lead to nothing good. He mounted and rode out of camp.

ONCE CLEAR OF THE HINDRANCES protecting the camp location, he hurried to the outskirts of the town and then slowed and entered behind buildings, he hoped unseen. Securing Gray in an alley, he stepped out onto the boardwalk to locate the coroner's office. Then he moved back into the shadows. Dusk creeping in would help hide him. He found a window in the rear of the coroner's office. Using his skinning knife, he threw the lock to the open position and raised the sash slowly, quietly, as he put the knife into the sheath that hung on his gun belt.

A quick listen told him this room was unoccupied. Noises from the other room confirmed the presence of someone in there. Likely the coroner. He climbed through the window opening, lowered the sash and went directly to the front door to lock it.

Half-sitting on the desk to face the door to the other room, Shawnee drew his bandana up over his nose and mouth. He waited in that position for a few minutes. The door opened. A small man in a stained white coat stepped in.

Meelee was sure right about the doc being mousey.

Dr. Janes took a step forward before he noticed Shawnee's presence. The sight startled him. "What—how did you get in here? What do you want?" His voice was shaky, nervous.

"Got a message for you," Shawnee said evenly.

"What—what message?"

"Mister Renquist sent me. Wants to make sure you're sticking to the agreement."

"What are you talking about? What agreement?"

He leaned away from the desk. "Come on, Doc, we both know what's going on here. He just wants to make sure you ain't going to slip up and say something out of turn. He knows you're under a lot of pressure. That's why he's paying you what he's paying you. Just wants to make sure you can stand up under it." Shawnee was fishing with these purposely chosen words, but he read in Janes's eyes that he was on the right track. He stopped talking there to allow Janes to digest and react.

Janes became more uneasy, wringing his hands. "I—I've done all right up to now. Why—?"

Shawnee cut him off. "'Cause he's paying you, that's why. He wants to be sure it ain't for naught."

Anxiety seemed to loosen Janes's tongue sooner than Shawnee had expected.

"Look here," Janes said. "I've done everything he asked. I covered up the truth about Banning. Now the Talkot thing as well. Why doesn't he trust me? What more does he want from me?"

Shawnee picked up on the Talkot reference and guessed that Renquist's hand was in that killing as well. Satisfied he'd gotten more from this than he'd planned, he decided it was time to leave. "Like I said, he just wants to be sure. I reckon you'll do all right."

Shawnee moved to the window and raised the sash. Then, looking back, he saw Janes breathing hard and touching a shaking hand to his forehead. "See you keep your mouth shut, Doc." He climbed out and trotted toward his horse.

Reviewing the information he had picked up from Janes as he rode away from Bodeen, Shawnee concluded that Renquist killed Foy's father, leading to his pay off to Janes to ensure an accidental death ruling. The reason Banning was killed in the first place was still unknown. Then, considering Talkot's killing, he speculated that maybe, just maybe, Renquist did it to frame Foy. It was a good fit. What better way to get Foy gone than to wrap him up in a murder charge?

This prompted Shawnee to add to his plan. He would pay a second visit in the same night, this time to Renquist. Time to shake things up even more. He'd need to be quick, though, before the doctor recovered enough sense to get with Renquist and blow this whole ruse to hell. Changing direction, he headed straight for the GR.

AFTER A HARD RIDE, SHAWNEE left Gray in a grove of trees a good distance away from the GR ranch house and covered the rest of the way on foot. There was activity in the bunkhouse. The hands were likely unwinding from the day's work. He passed carefully.

A few lights were visible in the main house but, for the most part, the place was quiet. He approached and stayed low and within the shadows, going to the side of the building. His objective was any open window he could find, preferably offering admission into a darkened room. In the back of the house, he found one. Opening it fully, he climbed into the room. Light streamed in from other sources through a partially open door, but there was enough darkness to allow him to remain hidden while he scanned the illuminated areas.

Along with the remote lighting, the smell of cigar smoke wafted in, likely coming from where Renquist was located. Shawnee moved slowly and quietly to the doorway. His view out showed him the parlor. Pressing himself against the wall, he observed the layout of the room. Renquist, facing the doorway, sat in an easy chair, puffing on that cigar.

Lifting the revolver from its holster, Shawnee stepped fully into the doorway, intending to be seen. He leveled the gun on Renquist. "Don't move!"

Renquist shot his gaze to the doorway. "Who are you?"

Shawnee took a step into the room. The light from the parlor shone on his entire figure as he faced the man. "No one you'd know."

"What do you want here?"

"Got a message for you."

"Well?"

"The coroner wants more money. Says you ain't paying him enough what with this Talkot thing now. He wants another two thousand or he ain't going to stand with you."

Shawnee's estimate of the money was a wild guess. Renquist's lack of surprise at the amount told him he was not far off.

"If I go down," Renquist said. "He goes down with me. I presume he's aware of that."

"He's gambling you won't let that happen."

"And what is your stake in this?"

"Doc's scared you'll put him down, so he made me his go-between. You pay him, he pays me a cut and I'm on my way. That's my stake in it."

"How do I know you're not working your own deal?"

"You don't. But I don't reckon you can chance that, can you?"

Renquist took a moment to consider. "I suppose not, but I will set my own terms. I'll do nothing here, tonight. If you want the money, meet me at the Sorrel Creek Dam tomorrow morning."

"Why there?"

"Because I say so. That is the only time and place I will do this. Take it or leave it."

Shawnee thought quickly. This was obviously a ruse to allow time for Renquist to set up some kind of a trap. If he balked now, he took the chance that Renquist would back out. That could set this whole thing back too far and put Foy in further danger. No, this had to be seen through. If it was a trap, so be it. And maybe he could spring a trap of his own. "All right. Have it your way. Just make sure you bring the money."

"Are we done here?".

"We're done. You just stay right there a couple or three minutes till I'm gone."

Shawnee backed out of the room and hurried back to the entry window, holstering his gun as he moved. A quick climb through put him in the outside darkness. He hurried into the bushes.

MEELEE FINISHED EXTINGUISHING THE SPIT fire, leaving the roasted meat open to the rising smoke. The hunger-inducing smell of the cooking process filled the air in the camp. She crouched at the campfire with the rifle resting across her lap. The crackling of the blaze combined with the wildlife noises around her almost sounded like a song to her. Her eyes were trained on the entrance to the camp, but the darkness obscured all but the close areas illuminated by the fire. Weird shapes caused by the flames danced against the surrounding rock faces. She chewed on her bottom lip as she waited for Shawnee to return.

She allowed her mind to drift to thoughts of Shawnee and the feelings she had developed for him in the very short time she had known him. He cared for her. That was evident in the way he treated her, the concern he showed for her. It was more than just the obligatory respect a man displayed for a woman. There was feeling there. She was certain of it. And, while she knew deep down that a relationship like this would probably never work, she took comfort in the fact that, in the short term, in his company, she felt safe, she felt whole.

Movement from beyond the entrance drew her attention to it. She levered a round into the chamber of the gun and strained to see through the darkness.

"Don't shoot," Shawnee said. "It's me. I'm coming in."

Meelee got to her feet and held the Winchester at the ready, just in case. Watching the darkness, she saw the fire light reflect on his face and clothing as he rode in. Then she lowered the rifle hammer to rest as he dismounted and went to her.

"You all right?"

"I am now." She smiled. "Are you?"

He smiled back and nodded. "Yeah, I'm fine. That coroner's in this up to his eyeballs. From what he said, looks like Renquist's paying him for the accident ruling on Foy's pa. Now Talkot's killing's being messed with. Renquist likely had something to do with that one as well. Look, I'm going to need your help."

"Yes, whatever I can do." Meelee set the rifle butt on the ground and straightened her stance.

"I need you to talk that deputy into going up to the dam tomorrow morning. I paid a call on Renquist tonight, after I left the doc. Told him he had to pay the doc more to keep things under wraps. Passed myself off as the collector, the go-between. He wants me to meet him at the dam in the morning. Likely planning something, but if we can get the deputy to listen in, maybe he'll hear enough to nail Renquist and clear Foy."

Meelee's face tightened into a resolute expression. "If I have to get him there at gunpoint, I will."

Shawnee took a step closer and reached toward her. Then he checked his movement. "Whoa, now, don't do nothing like that. Just tell him you seen Foy's partner up there snooping around. If he thinks it'll get him more on Foy, he'll go."

"All right. I'll leave at dawn."

"You come right back here when you're done, you hear? I want you safe as possible."

Her hand found his. "Shawnee, I—"

"'Fraid that ain't a good idea, Meelee."

She allowed her hand to fall, knowing he was absolutely right.

"Now, you get some sleep close to the fire there," he said as he pointed to a spot across the camp. "I'll do the same... yonder."

16

AS THE MORNING RAYS OF sun shone over Bodeen, Meelee rode quickly into the main street, stopping at the hitch rail near the jail. She scanned the scene, looking for the deputy but saw only townspeople going about their business. Dismounting, she lashed the reins to the rail and stepped onto the boardwalk.

There was a padlock on the door. She considered going to the rear of the small building to attempt a visit with Foy through the cell window. A glance up the street changed her mind as Driskill walked toward her.

She waited for him to arrive.

"You waiting on me?" The lawman asked as he reached her.

"Yes."

"Would have thought you'd seen enough of me yesterday."

She forced a smile. "You were just doing your job. I know that now. I came across something I think you'll be interested in."

"How's that?"

"I took a ride before sunup to clear my head. With all that's been going on of late, I'm having trouble sleeping. Anyway, I ended up at the dam. I saw that stranger, the one Foy was with before you arrested him. He was poking around up there. Seemed very interested in something up on the cliff. He was still there when I left. Maybe, if you question him, you can get more information on Foy. "

"You turned around right quick, didn't you? Thought you was friendly with Banning."

"I was, but if he broke the law, I don't want anything to do with him. I'm not going outside the law for anyone."

"Now you're making sense."

"Are you going up there?"

"I reckon so. Can't hurt none."

"Well, good luck."

Meelee pulled her reins free and mounted. Without another word, she directed her horse up the street in the direction she had come. The deputy turned and started toward the stable to get his horse.

Moments later, he rode out of town at a fairly fast clip. She sat mounted in an alley a few doors away from the jail, having doubled back to wait there. As Driskill passed, she moved out into the street and walked her horse until he was far enough away. Then she set out to follow him, maintaining his speed. As she rode, she recalled Shawnee's caution to return to camp immediately, but then she quickly discarded it in favor of this new plan, one she was making up as she went.

She pressed on.

SHAWNEE TOOK A WHILE LOCATING the dam. As good as he was at seeking things out, this was fresh country into which he had never ventured. He also exercised much care. He had run across *hombres* like Renquist before and had learned quickly not to trust them or put anything past them.

In the middle distance, the sound of water slapping against

something could be heard nearby. Likely it was the wind making ripples in the creek and the noise came from the dam wall stopping their travel. He drew rein at the path that led up to the cliff just forward of the dam. Foy had described this to him when he related the details of the dream.

Dismounting, Shawnee tied Gray off on a branch. He scanned the path and the section of cliff that was visible from this point of view, catching sight of the hindquarters of a saddle horse. Assuming Renquist was waiting for him, he started up the path. When he was half way up, a figure stepped out from the underbrush, gun drawn and leveled. The badge on his shirt glinted in the morning sunlight.

Phin Driskill stood his ground. "Don't move."

Caught in the open with no available cover, Shawnee froze. With no other option available, he raised his hands to shoulder level. Any other move would earn him a bullet.

Driskill moved cautiously toward Shawnee, scrutinizing his face. "Well, now, don't you look familiar. Got a handbill on you a while back. I study them, y'know, every last one of them. You're wanted all over the country, for all sorts of stuff, even murder. Pearce, I think... yeah, that's it, Pearce, Alonso Pearce. Well, Mister Alonzo Pearce, you're under arrest." Driskill reached Shawnee's revolver out of its holster. Without taking his gaze off Shawnee, he pushed the gun into his waistband and pulled out handcuffs. "Turn around."

Shawnee complied, allowing the deputy to secure his wrists behind his back. Then Driskill gripped the arm of his shirt and pulled him around to face his captor.

"Deputy Driskill." The call came from behind the lawman.

Shawnee recognized Renquist's voice.

Driskill appeared to know the voice as well, but he did not turn toward it. Instead, he kept his eyes on Shawnee.

"Mister Renquist," Driskill said over his shoulder. "What are you doing up here?"

"Well, I... I was inspecting the dam." Renquist approached, leading his horse.

Driskill remained in place, covering Shawnee.

"What brings you up here?" Renquist asked.

"I got word Banning's partner was sneaking around up here. Not sure if this is him, but he's wanted, anyhow, so I'm taking him in."

Renquist stepped beside Driskill, leading his horse. "That's good work. I'm impressed."

Driskill grinned at the compliment. "Reckon I'll get him on into Bodeen now."

"Well, I'm finished here. Why don't I ride in with you?"

"Sure," Driskill said. "I welcome the company. Mind keeping an eye on him while I get my horse?"

Renquist drew his revolver and trained it on Shawnee. "I don't mind at all."

Driskill stepped back into the bushes. Renquist took a step closer to Shawnee.

"So," he said in a harsh whisper. "It looks as if this didn't work out quite the way you planned, eh?"

Shawnee said nothing, staring directly into Renquist's eyes. A slight smile crossed Renquist's face.

Upon Driskill's return, they walked Shawnee back to Gray, got him mounted and started out.

From a safe location nearby, Meelee emerged from the seclusion of some bushes. She led her horse into the open and mounted. Turning in the opposite direction of the three men, she set out at a gallop.

ENTERING BODEEN'S MAIN STREET, RENQUIST and Driskill rode slowly, with Driskill leading Shawnee's horse behind them. Shawnee, his hands cuffed behind his back, rode uncomfortably, trying hard to figure a way out of this. As the party reached the saloon's location, Renquist pulled up. Driskill pulled rein a little further ahead.

"I know it's rather early, but after what has happened, I could stand a drink," Renquist said. "Will you join me?"

"No, thanks," Driskill said. "I got to get this one locked up safe and sound. Then I got some paperwork to get through."

"As you wish. Perhaps later."

"Yeah, maybe."

Driskill continued on toward the jail. As Shawnee rode passed, Renquist flashed a contented grin at him. Shawnee gave the appearance of ignoring the gesture, but inwardly he took it for the message it gave, he was exactly where Renquist wanted him.

Driskill drew rein at the hitch rail in front of the sheriff's office. Gray stopped just behind him. Dismounting, Driskill secured his mount to the rail and led Gray in beside it. He tied those reins off, then drew his sidearm and stood back a few feet from Shawnee. "Throw your leg over the saddle," he said to Shawnee. "And drop down. Don't you try nothing."

Shawnee complied silently.

"Go ahead on to the door," Driskill said.

Shawnee moved to the door and stopped. Driskill stepped close and produced the key to the padlock. He holstered his gun long enough to unlock the door, left the open lock hanging in the hasp and then redrew the revolver. His left hand opened the door and threw it back. "Inside."

Shawnee stepped in. Driskill followed him and quickly closed the door. He went to the desk and deposited Shawnee's revolver in the top drawer. Returning to Shawnee, he transferred his gun to his left hand and fished out another key to unlock the handcuffs. Then he went to the door to the room that housed the cell and opened it. "Go on in."

Shawnee rubbed his wrists where the cuffs had chafed his skin as he walked through the doorway.

Inside the cell, Foy came off his bunk and stood up at the sound of their entry. He stayed in front of the bunk.

"Take ahold of them bars," Driskill said to Shawnee. He pointed at the cell bars.

Shawnee moved to the cell and gripped the bars with both hands. Driskill lifted a metal ring with a single key on it from a nail on the nearby wall. He inserted the key into the cell door lock and opened it. "Inside. And don't try anything."

Shawnee complied. Driskill slammed and locked the door behind him and then exited and closed the room door.

"What happened?" Foy asked. "How did—?"

"I got skunked is what happened." Shawnee shook his head in disgust. "The one thing I didn't figure on, that deputy spotting me from a wanted poster. He threw down on me 'fore I had a chance to move."

Shawnee took a step to the bar protected window and looked out, searching for an escape route. He found none. "They feed you here?"

"You're thinking about food?" Foy sounded shocked. "Now?"

"No, I'm trying to figure a way out of here. What about the food?"

"The deputy brings it in."

"Well, so far, that's the only chance we got. We get him to open that door, maybe we can pull something."

"Pull what?"

"I don't know." Anger and distress were in Shawnee's voice. "I didn't figure on none of this shit and that's on me. Getting us out of here's on me, as well. One thing's sure, I ain't staying penned up like this for long."

Shawnee paced the length of the cell, already experiencing slight panic at the prospect of spending time in confinement. He took a seat on the opposite bunk and sat there for a long moment before speaking. "Sorry, kid. I ain't feeling all that proud of myself about now. And I get kind of *loco* when I'm in a fix like this here. No call to take it out on you. We got to work together."

"It's all right. I know."

RENQUIST SAT AT A TABLE in the saloon nursing a jigger of whiskey. During the hour he had been there, he observed the inhabitants carefully. At this time of day, the place was populated with no-accounts, drunkards, and a few miscreants. He saw here precisely what he sought, an easily led group. Fed enough liquor and incitement, they would willingly do his bidding, bidding they would come to view as ideas they'd conceived. He had already laid the groundwork earlier. Speaking of the high regard in which he held Brent Talkot, he alluded to the fact that it was a shame that Brent's killer was not being punished. Simply sitting in a cell was definitely not a penalty. A trial would only give him the chance to get off. Something ought to be done about it.

They were already conferring in small groups. Now all that remained was to fire them up to the point at which mob mentality would overtake them. Then he could stand back and allow his plan to unfold.

He got up and circulated among the factions, speaking quietly and privately as he moved. "It is not right that Brent's killer just sits there in that cell."

"Some lawyer will probably get him off without punishment," he said to another.

"His helper is just as guilty," he suggested later.

A further statement here and there, coupled with the purchase of more drinks for those interested, stoked about fifteen of them to engage in combined discussions of the validity of their newly embraced purpose. From there, it was an easy task to assemble them into one well-fueled pack, anxious to do that which Renquist orchestrated, but that which they considered their own.

Then someone stepped outside and grabbed a rope from a saddle. Drunken fingers fumbled with attempts to fashion a hangman's noose. Finally, one man figured it out and was still sober enough to accomplish it. Cheers went up from the rest, congratulating the man.

More liquor was plied. More encouragement came from Renquist. The crowd became noisier, more raucous. Cries of "Let's get 'em!" went up from several. Then, as one, they poured through the batwings and started up the middle of the street toward the jail, leaving Renquist alone in the saloon.

He waited a few minutes. Then he slipped out into the street and went straight to his horse. He mounted and headed slowly out of town, taking the direction opposite to the path followed by the mob.

THE CROWD CLOSED ON THE jail, shouting demands and threats. It became loud enough to cause Driskill to rise from his desk and move quickly to the barred window. His look outside sent a chill up his spine. This promised to be a problem. He watched them gather boisterously in the middle of the street. They milled around, working themselves up to action

Turning to the gun rack behind the desk, Driskill pulled down a double-barrel shotgun. Then, hearing a call from outside for him to turn his prisoners over, he grabbed a box of shells from a desk drawer and broke and loaded the weapon. He closed the gun, stuffed several shells into his shirt pocket and went to the door.

Pulling in a deep breath to steady himself, he threw the door open and stepped resolutely through the doorway. The crowd reached the center of the street. He held the shotgun shouldered, ready to fire. They stopped.

Holding the gun in place, Driskill reached behind him and pulled the door closed. He took a step forward and assumed an aggressive firing stance. The weapon was pointed at the center of the group as they stood in haphazard order. "That's far enough!"

"We want them prisoners," the man with the rope shouted.

Driskill moved his point of aim to that man. "I don't give a shit what you want. They're in my custody and they're staying that way. Now, all of you, back off!"

"We taking them, even if'n we got to walk over you to do it," the man said loudly.

The others seemed energized by this statement and again started moving forward.

Driskill's next words stopped them. "This is loaded with scatter-shot and I'm within my rights to use it. Now you men get out of here 'fore I cut loose on you."

There followed a few seconds of silence as both Driskill and the mob stood their ground. Then someone from one side of the group called out, "You can't get all of us."

This was enough to draw Driskill's attention to that man. From the opposite side, a fist sized stone was thrown. It hit Driskill just behind the ear and below the line of his hat. He yelped and faltered, collapsing to one knee. The shotgun, still in his grip, fell away from his shoulder.

The group began to close on him. As they advanced, their confidence increased. They moved faster.

As the mob came to the edge of the boardwalk, almost close enough to grab Driskill, a rifle fired. Their attention was shifted away from Driskill toward the perceived location of the shot.

Meelee stepped from the corner of the building, her Winchester aimed at the crowd with the hammer cocked and her finger on the trigger. "Stop!" she shouted. "Stand still! I'll shoot anyone that moves. I mean it."

Keeping the gun trained on the men, she moved close to Driskill as he looked up to acknowledge her presence. "Deputy," she said without taking her eyes off her aim. "Can you get up?"

These few seconds had been enough for the deputy to recover a little. There was pain and dizziness, and he felt like he was going to puke, but he was determined to hold out. "Yes, ma'am." This sounded more like a grunt as he forced himself up on shaky limbs.

Immediately, he lifted the shotgun to firing position and stood shoulder to shoulder with Meelee. For a moment, they stood staring their adversaries down as Driskill read the tenor of the group. Then he spoke to Meelee quietly, "They ain't backing down. You head inside. I'll cover you."

Meelee backed up to the jail door while keeping her rifle aimed at the crowd. Only when she felt the door behind her did she lower the gun and quickly let herself inside. Clearing the doorway, she turned and lifted the weapon back to its firing position.

"I'm in," she called to Driskill. "Come on."

Driskill stepped back, maintaining his bead on the mob. Once inside, he slammed the door shut. Then he reached for the wooden barricade leaning against the wall and inserted it in the metal slots on the sides of the door frame. "That should hold it," he said as he lowered the shotgun.

Meelee lowered her rifle and slipped the hammer forward gently, resting it on the live round in the chamber.

As Driskill turned to Meelee, the effects of his wound took over, causing him to fall against the door. Over shouts and pounding by the mob, Meelee dropped her rifle on the floor and went to Driskill. She pulled his arm over her shoulder and placed her other arm around his waist to support him as he tried to regain balance. She struggled under his weight as she walked him to the chair behind the desk, then helped him to sit down.

A stone crashed through the window and bounced heavily on the floor near her feet. She picked up the rifle and poked the muzzle through the hole in the glass. Without aiming, she pulled the hammer back and fired one shot into the crowd. Driskill watched as she stared through the window at the mad scramble going on outside. She let out an angry yell.

17

MEELEE TURNED FROM THE WINDOW as the mob dispersed. In front of her, Driskill sat at the desk with his elbows placed on the surface and his head buried in his hands. Blood dripped from behind his ear onto his hand and then onto the desk. It was obvious to her that he was in pain and that the wound may be worse than she first thought. She went to him and stood the rifle against the desk. He had pushed his hat away, making the cut more visible. Leaning forward, she inspected it more carefully.

"That looks kind of bad," she said uncertainly.

"It hurts something fierce. Can't clear my head. Everything's whirling around."

"Where is the cell key?"

"What do you want that for?"

"Foy knows doctoring. He knows a lot about injuries. I think he can help you."

"He's a prisoner."

Meelee crouched at Driskill's side. "You can trust him. He didn't kill Talkot. He didn't even know him. The only reason he surrendered to you was to keep you from arresting me. Let me release him so he can help you."

Meelee allowed Driskill the time he needed to think this through. Finally, he pointed. "Key's in that drawer."

Meelee moved around behind him to the drawer he had indicated and opened it. The key was there, next to the revolver he had confiscated from her. She noted its presence, then ignored it and picked up the key. Going quickly through the door that led to the cell, she inserted the key and turned the lock as Foy and Shawnee moved toward her.

"Meelee," Foy said. "What are you doing here? What's going on? What were those shots?"

She pulled the cell door open. "That was me. There were some men outside trying to lynch you both. I helped the deputy drive them off, but he's hurt. I don't like the looks of his wound and I don't know what to do for him. Can you help him?"

Foy took a second to digest the request. Then he reacted as she expected. "Of course. Where is he?"

"He's at the desk. He says he can't clear his head."

Foy moved past her and went into the office. Meelee looked at Shawnee, who still stood in the center of the cell.

She read his thoughts and spoke before he could. "I know. You told me to stay at camp, but I had to do something."

Shawnee smiled. "Kind of glad you did."

They entered the main room as Foy reached Driskill and bent to observe the wound.

"What hit you?"

"Must a been a rock or something. Hurts like hell. Can't seem to get my head to stop spinning. Feels like I got to heave my guts out."

Foy went behind him. "I'm going to pull your chair back. I want you to lean forward slowly, with your head between your legs. Stay that way while I dress the wound."

When the deputy did as instructed, Foy looked around the office something he could use to clean and bind the cut. He found a pitcher of water and a basin, but no cloth. Pulling Driskill's shirt tail from inside his pants, he tore strips from the bottom. "This'll have to do. Sorry about the shirt."

"I ain't that partial to it," Driskill mumbled.

Foy used the shirt strips to cleanse the blood away. Driskill winced several times during the process but remained still. Finally, Foy wrapped a piece of the cloth around the deputy's head in an attempt to cover the open area.

While this went on, Meelee kept watch at the window.

"How do you feel now?" Foy asked when he was finished.

"A little better. Thanks."

"Stay there till your head is completely clear. It might take a while."

More time elapsed. Driskill slowly raised his head and seemed to have recovered enough to be able to function. He looked across the room at Foy. "Thanks for what you done," he grunted. "But, I got to tell you, you're still in custody."

"I know," Foy said. "I'm not going anywhere."

"What about your friend there?"

"I can't speak for him."

Standing beside Foy, Shawnee spoke up. "Safer in here than out there, I reckon. I'll set a spell."

"Can't trust these folks hereabouts," Driskill said. "Can't protect you here. I got to get you up to Denver. I figure we'll wait here till dark and then head out. I don't expect them idiots'll follow us."

"They'll probably be too drunk by that time to do anything," Meelee said from the window.

"That's what I'm counting on," Driskill said. "Ma'am, when it's dark enough, can I ask you to get the horses and bring them around back? I'd do it, but I don't feel good leaving these two alone. It ain't safe. 'Sides, I ain't that steady on my pins yet."

"I'll go." Meelee agreed.

"We do this right," Shawnee said. "They'll never know we lit out."

WHEN DARKNESS ARRIVED, DRISKILL OPENED the desk drawer and lifted Meelee's revolver out. He rose, then hesitated for a moment while he steadied himself. He crossed to the window at which Meelee had spent hours watching for activity in the street. She looked around as he reached her.

"You might need this," he said, handing the gun over.

She made no reply as she dropped the weapon into the vacant holster on her hip.

"Don't show yourself," Driskill said. "Stay in the shadows and behind buildings."

Taking in one long breath, Meelee exhaled hard and went to the door. She caught the looks both Foy and Shawnee flashed at her, gave them a weak smile and exited quickly.

Heeding Driskill's instructions, she ducked into the first alley she reached and used the areas behind the buildings to make her way to the livery stable. She stopped briefly on the way to note the noise coming from the saloon across the street from her. Confident that the mob would continue drinking itself into oblivion, she moved on.

Thankful for the fact that the stable was on her side of the street, negating the need to cross in the open, she quietly slipped around the corner of the building and inside through the open doorway. Moving directly into the darkened areas of the stable, she looked around for the attendant. No one was there.

Satisfied she was alone, Meelee went about saddling the three horses. She led them out of the building and into the alley. It was a narrow area, requiring her to move the animals through it one at a time. As she went back through and began leading the last one, she heard footsteps on the boardwalk. She stopped and tried to keep the horse quiet by placing her hand over its muzzle. The person passed without taking notice. Breathing a sigh of relief, she continued the journey to the back of the jail and tied the horses off next to her own.

She moved quickly through the alley to the door. Her soft knock was answered by Foy. He opened the door to admit her.

Driskill looked up from the desk. "How is it out there?"

"Quiet," Meelee said. "Except for the saloon. They're having a grand old time in there."

"That's good," Driskill said. "The drunker they get, the less of a threat they'll be." He stood up and again waited a second to be sure of his stability, ready to support himself on the desk if it became necessary. Satisfied, he verified the loads in his revolver and placed Shawnee's gun in his waistband. "We ought to get to getting while we still can."

He took a step closer to Foy. "I'm saving your life by doing this. I hope you've got the good sense to cooperate."

"I won't be a problem," Foy said.

"I'm going with you," Meelee broke in as she lifted the rifle from its position against the wall.

"Now hold on a minute," Driskill said, turning to her. "That wasn't part of the plan."

Thumbs hooked in his belt, Shawnee shook his head. "You leave her here, you might could be signing her death warrant. No telling how hot them boys'll be, they find us gone."

Driskill paused to consider this.

"You want that on your head?"

Driskill sighed. "Reckon you're right. Can't take that chance. Ma'am, where's your horse?"

"Out back with the others."

"Then you'll be coming with us. Let's ride."

They exited onto the street quickly, keeping to the shadows and filing into the alley leading to the back of the jail. Lack of illumination on the street, with the exception of dim light coming from adjacent businesses, facilitated their attempt to hide their movements. Mounting quickly, they went to an immediate gallop away from the jail.

LOCKE'S RIDE WAS SWIFT, HARD and direct. He had stood at his post across the street from the sheriff's office, watching and waiting, after being ordered there by Renquist.

As the deputy, his two prisoners, and the woman had exited the building and moved quickly into the alley, Locke had crossed the street and carefully entered the alley. He kept hidden and observed them mounting waiting horses and hurrying away. Immediately aware of their intent, he trotted across to his own horse, swung on and headed out of town. Now, a short time later, he thundered into the quiet GR Ranch area and stopped at the main house. Dropping from the saddle, he bounded up onto the porch and rapped heavily on the door.

Renquist himself answered the knock. "What news?"

"They ducked out, all four of 'em, and headed north," Locke said quickly. "Likely heading for Denver."

"What happened to the lynching?"

"Reckon it didn't work. That woman showed up just when they

was taking the deputy down. The two of 'em buffaloed the mob and run them off. They're useless now, drunk as a skunk."

Renquist thought for a second. "If they make it to Denver, we will never be able to get to them. Roust the men out. Run those four down on the trail. No one lives. Make it look like they were lynched. Go!"

He turned and ran toward the bunkhouse.

———

DRISKILL LED HIS PARTY SWIFTLY away from the jail. They maintained their speed for several miles until Driskill, in an attempt to keep from exhausting the horses, slowed them down and placed Foy and Shawnee in the lead where they would always be in his sight.

Meelee rode beside Driskill for a few miles, then she moved forward to side Shawnee, leaving the deputy to ride alone. He watched as they smiled at each other, but this did not distract him from his vigilance. They were still his prisoners and would be treated as such until they reached Denver. At the same time, the danger of attack by a crazed bunch of citizens, however remote, still existed. It would be folly to ignore that threat.

They proceeded in this manner for a couple hours at which point Shawnee raised his hand to signal a halt. The party stopped.

"Why'd you stop?" Driskill asked.

"I got a funny feeling we ain't alone out here," Shawnee said, looking at the country around them.

"What do you see?"

"Don't see nothing. Don't hear nothing, neither." He shrugged. "Just a feeling I got."

Driskill pondered this for a few seconds. "We won't take no chances." He scanned the area himself. "Head for the trees there. We'll hole up there a mite and rest the horses. Anybody's out there, we should be able to spot them pretty soon."

They turned their horses off the trail and entered a stand of cottonwood trees. The low growth of the forest afforded adequate concealment. Here they dismounted.

Shawnee poured canteen water into his hat as a receptacle to water Gray.

Driskill stepped to a spot from which he could observe the trail. He remained there for a few moments and then, seeing nothing, returned to the others.

He duplicated Shawnee's action to water his own horse. Then they proceeded to water Foy's and Meelee's animals. As Driskill finished with Meelee's horse, he felt a presence behind him. He had let his guard down now realized that fact. He reacted by turning, but did so too late. Shawnee had already snatched the deputy's gun from its holster. Driskill dropped his hat and made a move for the revolver stashed in his belt.

"Don't!"

Driskill saw no other option but to submit. He raised his hands to shoulder level.

"Now, deputy, you're going to listen to me," Shawnee pulled the gun from Driskill's belt. "Foy didn't kill Talkot. Renquist done that, and he done Foy's pa in, too. When Foy got too close to finding that out, Renquist killed Talkot to frame Foy to get him off the trail. I know Foy's pa got killed intentional, 'cause I dug up his grave and seen he was slugged in the back of the head. It's the only wound he got from behind. Everything else is in the front and come from the fall. That whack is likely why he went over that cliff in the first place, and it's likely what killed him. Renquist paid the coroner off to say it was an accident. Renquist's your killer sure as I'm breathing. I ain't letting Foy hang for something he ain't done."

Driskill stood there, listening, letting it all sink in. It was a lot to digest. His years as a lawman had taught him to listen well and to weigh the information and its source. Pearce's statement could hold water. What made it more believable was the fact that the man was still here. With his freedom at stake, Pearce was committed enough to this to stay, instead of running, and to stand up for his friend.

Maybe there was some validity to what he said.

In a last effort to shake their story, Driskill presented the only counter arguments he could come up with. "What about Banning's fight with Talkot?"

"Who told you I fought with Talkot?" Foy asked.

"Renquist. Said he seen it."

"He made that up. I never even met the man."

"And the rifle, the one that killed Talkot? I found that in your hotel room, hid under the bed."

"It's not mine. I don't own a gun of any kind."

Shawnee broke in with the obvious question. "How'd you come to look in Foy's room anyhow?"

"Renquist. He said he saw Banning with the rifle."

"Well, there you go. I'm telling you, Renquist set this whole thing up to get rid of Foy. What I ain't figured out yet is why he killed Foy's pa in the first place."

"I think it had something to do with the dam," Foy said. "Why else would they have been up there on that cliff when it happened?"

"I'd say that's one for Renquist to answer," Shawnee said.

Driskill continued to ponder this. As far-fetched as it sounded, it still seemed plausible. And the people telling it made sense. They both could have cut and run as soon as Pearce grabbed that gun, but they were still here, arguing their case. That had to count for something. He lowered his hands slowly and turned to face them. "I believe you."

"You sure you ain't just saying that 'cause I got the drop on you?" Shawnee asked.

"No. As *loco* as it sounds, what you say makes sense."

"Well, finally." Shawnee grinned. "Now, what are we going to do to make this right?"

"Wait!" Meelee broke in. "I hear something."

They stopped to listen. The sound of horses approaching reached their ears.

"I knew I smelled something wrong," Shawnee said.

"Likely that bunch from Bodeen," Driskill said.

"It couldn't be," Meelee said. "They were too drunk to stand up, much less ride."

Shawnee's assessment was ominous. "It's Renquist's men, I'll bet on it. He needs us all dead to survive."

18

NINE MEN RODE ALONG THE trail two hundred yards from the trees that kept the deputy and his companions hidden. With a full moon shining over the area, the man in the lead had no trouble following the tracks left by the four horses. When they reached the point at which Driskill had led his party off the road, the leader called a halt. The others grouped around him. The lead man pointed toward the treeline.

From a crouching position, shielded by a cottonwood, Shawnee observed the group as they dismounted and started moving toward the woods. The deputy went to a knee beside him.

"Too late to run," Shawnee said. "We got good cover in here. I say we stand and fight. Hit them before they can spot us."

"Sounds about right."

Shawnee handed Driskill his revolver and got up to join Foy and Meelee where they stood with the horses. "Going to be some lead flying around here. Tie the horses off back a ways and stay with them."

"Give me a gun. I can help," Foy said.

"We both can," Meelee handed Foy the rifle from the saddle holster and drew her sidearm.

"No time to argue," Shawnee said. "See to the horses."

Meelee took on that job, leading the horses several yards farther into the trees and off to the side. Selecting an area where they were out of the line of fire, she secured them to a stout branch and then rejoined the others.

Foy and Shawnee moved quickly back to where Driskill knelt.

"You all right using that?" Shawnee asked Foy, indicating the Winchester lever-action.

"Yeah. I said I don't *own* a gun. Never said I can't use one."

They each took cover behind a separate tree, spread out in a skirmish line, presenting a united front facing the trail.

Shawnee watched as Renquist's men drew their weapons and approached the tree line. He brought his revolver up to firing position, cocked it, and fired. The bullet hit one of the men in the shoulder, dropping him out of action. Caught in the open, the rest scattered and went to prone positions. They opened defensive fire.

Driskill matched Shawnee shot for shot, going through three rounds each. Meelee joined in, expending two more. None of them hit a mark, but they kept the attackers at bay. They also drew more return fire, prompting Renquist's men to waste more ammunition than was prudent.

Foy levered a round into the Winchester, hesitated for a second and then fired into the group. A yelp came from the target area, but darkness shrouded the result.

"Good shot." Shawnee's vantage point afforded him sight of the hit.

Foy fired another shot, hitting nothing.

Clouds rolled in to cover the moon, reducing illumination. The next round of shots were fired without having targets, simply to keep the attackers' heads down.

The GR crew stayed on the ground and tried to crawl to the cover of some small boulders along the side of the road. Shawnee saw the outlines of three men make the move successfully, leaving four men still unprotected on the ground.

Three of those men tried the sprint. Each was hit by at least one round fired from the trees.

The fourth man made his run for the boulders just as the moon reappeared from behind the clouds. A round from Foy's rifle took that man down.

The remaining three aggressors, safe in the rocks, tried to lay down a barrage, but the obscurity of their targets succeeded only in chipping chunks from the trees. While those behind the trees rationed their ammunition and picked their shots, the GR hands were not as wise and soon found themselves running dry. Their gunfire ceased.

Seconds later, the sound, then the sight of the attackers was detected as they reached their horses, mounted and quickly left rode out.

"Reckon they give up." Shawnee stepped from behind the tree. The others peeked out from their concealments. The last sound was that of the fading hoofbeats. Then quiet descended over the area.

Shawnee and Driskill moved slowly out of the treeline toward their fallen attackers, guns at the ready, to check the condition of each of the wounded men. Foy checked on Meelee, finding her unhurt, before joining them.

"Well, we got two dead, another one on his way and there's one hit in the arm," Driskill said.

"I'll try to help the wounded."

"They made their choice, Foy," Shawnee shook his head. "They take what they get."

"Sorry, Shawnee I don't see it that way." Foy went to a knee beside the mortally wounded man to find a chest wound that seriously hampered the man's breathing. He tried to make him comfortable, but there was nothing more he could do, and he soon expired.

Shawnee watched with respect as the boy conducted his examination. He would have just let the cur lie there and bleed for the fact that the man had tried to kill him. Yet Foy had helped him all the same.

Foy remained on a knee beside the dead man for a few seconds, then he moved to the other man. As he worked, he announced that this was only a flesh wound. The bullet had merely taken a chunk from the man's arm. Using pieces from the man's shirt, he bound the arm and advised him to see a doctor as soon as possible.

Driskill interrupted. "You go find that doctor somewheres far from these parts, you hear? And you do it right quick. You can count yourself lucky I got better things to do than arrest you. Now, git!"

The man got up and headed in the direction of his grazing horse. He did not look back.

While watching the man walk away, Driskill's attention was off his prisoners.

"Deputy," Shawnee said quietly.

Driskill turned to find Shawnee again holding a gun on him.

"Just making sure we don't lose track of what was said a spell back."

Driskill raised his hands to just above his waist to indicate a halt. "I told you I believe you. You're closer to this than I am. What do you think we should do?"

Shawnee holstered his weapon. As he spoke, he picked up two of the attacker's guns and inserted them in his waistband. "That coroner's the key to this whole mess. We need to shake him loose. If we can get him to turn on Renquist, we can nail Renquist and clear Foy. But we got to do it quick-like. Renquist finds out we're still breathing, he'll figure out our play and go after the coroner. He'll look to take out anyone that can hurt him. Way I see it, you scare the be-jesus out of the coroner, get him to talk. While you're doing that, me and Foy'll pick up Renquist. That way he can't get to the coroner."

"Sounds like it'll work."

"Then let's get to moving. We ain't got much time."

The trio started moving back toward the trees to get their horses.

"Hey, what about me?" Meelee said.

Foy stopped and turned back to Meelee. "You should stay with the deputy. You'll be safer."

"He's right," Driskill said. "Besides, you'll be a witness to whatever the coroner spills."

Meelee joined them and they continued back into the treeline.

LOCKE LED HIS MEN INTO the GR Ranch main area about an hour before dawn. They pulled up sharply at the ranch house and Locke dropped heavily out of the saddle. He climbed up on the porch, preparing to knock, when the door opened abruptly.

In the doorway, Renquist stood fully clothed. Observing that their numbers had been pared by half, he stepped to within six inches of Locke. "What happened?"

"I don't know," Locke said. "They must have seed us coming. They ambushed us and dropped us like flies. We're all that's left."

"And they're *alive?*" Renquist's anger increased his voice to a shout.

"Yeah. We couldn't get to 'em."

"Fools! Damn fools! How hard was this?"

Renquist ran his hand across the back of his head and paced, in frantic thought. He continued to pace, calming himself before speaking as if he was thinking to himself. "The men you left behind will be identified as my employees. That will convince the deputy I'm involved. He will come here with questions, questions I do *not* want to answer. Savvy?" He stopped pacing and faced them. "Get more guns, more ammunition Take up positions around the house here. No one gets past you. No one gets in. Now move!"

The men dismounted and ran for the bunkhouse to replenish their arms. Locke turned to follow them.

"Not you," Renquist said.

Locke stopped.

"You get a fresh horse and ride to Bodeen. Kill that damn coroner. I don't care how you do it, I want him dead. *Dead,* you understand?"

"Yeah."

"Then go!"

Locke moved quickly to carry out the order as Renquist went back inside and proceeded to his gun cabinet. He had to be ready.

DAWN BROKE THROUGH, SHEDDING LIGHT and brightening the sky over Bodeen as Meelee and Driskill reached the outskirts of the town. They'd ridden through the night and never broke stride. They now directed their horses at full gallop into the main street and went directly to the coroner's office. Driskill, with Meelee close behind him, led the way up the side staircase to the living quarters above, occupied by Dr. Janes. He rapped hard and loud on the door and kept it up until a semi-awake physician, in his robe and slippers, opened the door.

"Yes, what is it?" Janes asked sleepily.

"Official business," Driskill said, brushing past the man.

Meelee entered behind the deputy and closed the door. Janes backed away from them. Before Driskill could begin his interrogation, Meelee broke in.

"How much is that bastard Renquist paying you to cover up Jeremy Banning's murder?"

Janes's expression showed surprise. "What? What the hell are you talking about?"

Driskill picked it up from there. "While you're at it, explain how you can be so sure the ball that killed Brent Talkot was a four-fifty-one. It didn't dawn on me when I read your report, but lead balls get pretty mangled up once they hit a body. Yet you had no problem gauging it. Four-fifty-one, not even a maybe."

"What is all this? How dare you question me like this. You have no call to—"

"I got *every* call, Doc. I'm trying to solve a murder here, two murders, truth be told. Now, you're going to answer my questions straight up or I'll arrest you as an accessory after the fact in both murders." Driskill paused for a moment to let his words sink in. He watched as Janes became increasingly nervous, chewing on his lower lip and wringing his hands. After the silence, he continued. "When you did the autopsy on Jeremy Banning, did you find anything on the body showing he might have got hit from behind?"

"No."

"You seem awful sure of that. You sure there wasn't a hole in the back of the skull like he was slugged with something hard? Hell, that was ten years ago, but you didn't even think about it. You knew exactly what to say."

"I... I have a very good memory. It's my work. Of course I remember it."

"I ain't buying it. I got a witness that says that mark's there. That means Banning was murdered. And it means you covered it up, ruled it an accident when it wasn't. Now, like Miss Scocroft asked a minute ago, what's Renquist paying you to keep this under wraps?"

Janes became completely rattled. "I didn't.... He's not.... It was an accident. Banning died from a fall. I never authorized an exhumation."

"I never said nothing about that. I just said I got a witness. Now, you better start talking straight—"

"You can't cross examine me like this," Janes said, finally finding some grit. "I've done nothing. I'm not saying another word."

"I'll let you ponder a spell, think about where this is going. And where you're going. Meantime, get some clothes on. We're going downstairs. I want to see that four-fifty-one ball for myself, see how that measures out."

Driskill watched as Janes went toward the next room. He followed him in and stood in the doorway while the doctor pulled on a pair of pants. Putting his arms through the suspenders, he pulled them over his shoulders and sat to get his shoes on.

"Close enough," Driskill said. "Let's go."

Silently, Janes led the way to the apartment door and stepped out onto the staircase. Driskill and Meelee followed in single file with Meelee in the rear. About halfway down the stairs, a shot sounded. At the same time, a bullet slammed into the wall just above Janes's head. The doctor ducked and cringed as Driskill and Meelee pulled their weapons.

The puff of powder smoke rising over the alley across the street indicated the assailant's position. As he cocked his revolver and aimed a second shot at Janes, Driskill and Meelee both fired more rounds into the alley. He stumbled out of the alley a second later and dropped heavily on the boardwalk. His body twitched noticeably and then stopped moving.

"Watch him," Driskill told Meelee.

He climbed around the doctor and hurried down the stairs.

Meelee, her gun still in her hand, grabbed Janes's shirt and tugged on it. "Go on down. Get off the stairs."

Janes stumbled his way down.

Driskill hurried across the street to examine the attacker. Satisfied that the man was dead, he noted the entry of two bullets, one in the chest, one in the stomach. He recognized the dead man as Locke, Renquist's man who'd fetched him from Denver.

Trotting back across the street, he met Meelee and Janes as they reached the street. Meelee still had a hold on Janes's shirt.

"Dead." Driskill directed his next words to Janes. "I reckon I don't have to tell you that shot was meant for you. And he was working for Renquist. You about ready to talk to me now?"

"Y-Yes," Janes's voice and body trembled.

"Get inside, case he wasn't alone."

Janes produced a key to the office door and fumbled to work it. Meelee took it from him and unlocked and opened the door. They stepped inside. Janes was still shaking.

Meelee spoke quietly to Driskill. "Did... did my shot hit that man?"

"He's got two holes in him. I didn't fire but one shot."

"Oh." Meelee's voice sounded noticeably shaken.

"Don't worry," Driskill said. "You didn't do nothing wrong. I'll back you up."

Meelee was pensive. "That's not what concerns me."

19

SUNLIGHT BRIGHTENED THE COUNTRYSIDE AS night gave way to morning. The GR ranch house area was quiet. Renquist's three designated protectors were placed strategically, one at each side of the house and one on the porch. The two on the sides each used rain barrels for cover while the guard on the porch crouched behind a hay bale placed there for that purpose. Their positions were set up to repel a frontal assault. This conformed to Renquist's belief that his adversaries would approach straight on. While he had changed his expectation to include at least Banning instead of Driskill alone, he discounted a rear tactic. He did not give them credit for the resourcefulness necessary to conceive and enact a plan of any intricacy.

The guards stayed vigilant while, inside the house, Renquist paced around the parlor floor. Rifle in hand, he periodically checked the area through the front window. His vision of the outcome of this situation was that he would prevail as he always had. Even with as few as three defenders, he would easily vanquish his enemies due to his superior intelligence. Any of those who might survive would rue the day they went against him.

FOY AND SHAWNEE CRESTED A hill above the ranchhouse and halted to survey the scene below them. They had a full view of the rear of the house but were not close enough to spot the guards.

"Got to figure them waddies made it back here last night," Shawnee mused. "Reckon they'll be waiting for us."

"How do we do this?"

"You get around front and get to cover. Let Renquist know you're coming for him. Make a real ruckus. That'll draw their fire and keep their attention on you. And it'll show me where they're at so's I can take them out, one by one."

"All right, but leave Renquist to me."

"Uh-huh, but you watch him. *Hombres* like him usually got a lot of tricks to fall back on."

They continued their approach but took a route that put them in front of the ranch house while they remained out of sight. This took longer, but it kept them safe and hidden. After circling the area, they dismounted and secured their horses far enough away to keep them out of sight. Shawnee opened his saddlebag and pulled out the two revolvers he had lifted from the scene of the previous night's attack. He handed them to Foy. Foy jammed the revolvers into his waistband. Shawnee went back into the saddlebag and found a box of ammunition and then pulled the rifle from Gray's saddle scabbard. Foy took both from him. They moved forward on foot, keeping to the bushes. At the selected spot, they crouched.

"Keep your shots high," Shawnee said. "You got enough fire power here to keep their heads down a spell. Give me a couple minutes to get around and come in from behind, then cut loose. I'm betting Renquist's inside. There's a window on the west side of the house that gets you in without being seen. That'll get you to Renquist. I'll clear that side first. Head for the window when you can."

Foy took a deep breath.

Shawnee detected hesitation. "You can do this."

"Yeah, I can."

Shawnee patted him on the shoulder and moved quietly into thicker brush. In an instant, he was gone from sight.

Foy waited a tense few minutes and then put his part of the plan in action. His voice resounded in the still morning air. "Renquist, it's Foy Banning. I know what you did. I'm coming for you."

He fired one shot from one of the revolvers and shifted his position, certain the powder smoke would pinpoint his location. Almost instantly, return fire came from the three spots occupied by the guards.

Foy watched as Shawnee moved on the man crouched behind the barrel at the forward corner of west side of the house. Foy kept up a rapid barrage to hold the man's attention. Keeping low, Shawnee trotted behind the man and approached with revolver drawn. He made it to within two feet of the shooter before the man sensed a presence behind him and turned. Shawnee raised his gun and swung it hard, hitting the man's head. The man folded and dropped to the ground. Immediately, Shawnee turned and hurried toward the rear of the house.

Foy continually shifted to different spots to make a more difficult target as he emptied one revolver and engaged the second. Noticing the absence of shots from the west corner, he directed his fire at the remaining active locations to keep them busy. When he was certain Shawnee was out of the line of fire, he dropped the empty revolver and, picking up the rifle, moved in a low profile trot toward the west corner of the building. Keeping to a wide arc, he stayed under the cover of bushes until he was on the side of the building, out of the guards' fields of vision. He moved in from there to the window Shawnee had described. Finding it unlocked, he lifted the sash and climbed in.

SHAWNEE CIRCLED THE HOUSE AND moved on the shooter at the east corner. The cessation of gunfire from the bushes indicated Foy was on the move.

This guard's senses were sharper. He turned as Shawnee was half way to him and fired a wild shot. Shawnee instantly returned fire, his bullet piercing the man's chest. The man dropped his gun, grabbed his chest and fell, knocking the rain barrel over.

Moving in quickly, Shawnee kicked the gun away. A cursory look told him the shooter was no longer a threat, that his death was imminent. One less to cause trouble.

The man on the porch turned in Shawnee's direction. Shawnee reacted to this movement and made a dive for the protection of the building wall. A shot took a chunk out of the corner molding as he hit the wall and pressed his back against it. His assailant immediately made the same move against the adjacent wall. Both began inching forward to gain the shooting advantage.

Shawnee estimated his opponent's location. Figuring for the height of the porch, he pegged the man's legs to be about where his own waist was. Transferring his gun to his left hand, he turned the front of his body against the wall. Reaching around the corner, he fired blindly at where he gauged the legs to be and heard the scream as his bullet, at close range, bored its way into the man. This was followed by the sound of the body hitting the floor.

He rounded the corner with his gun still in his left hand. The man clutched at the wound in his upper leg as blood coursed from it. At the sight of his attacker, he tried to bring his revolver into play, but Shawnee fired again, hitting him in the lower jaw. The slug tore sideways through the top of his head, killing him instantly.

FOY MOVED CAUTIOUSLY THROUGH THE room to the parlor. Renquist stood ready at the window, his back to Foy.

"Don't move, Renquist." He leveled the rifle near his hip. "Toss your gun away."

Foy's gun was aimed at Renquist's back. Renquist tensed and heaved his weapon across the room. It clattered on the floor as he raised his hands to shoulder height.

"Are you going to kill me, Banning?" Renquist asked ominously, without turning. "If you are, you'd better get to it because, given the chance, I *will* kill you."

"I know you killed my father."

"Yes, I did, didn't I? And he made it so easy." Renquist seemed to be almost gloating, proud of his accomplishment. "He was such a trusting soul. I almost hated to do it, but it had to be."

"Tell me why—why you did it. Then maybe I'll let you live." Without realizing it, Foy, totally consumed by this, took a step closer.

"So I can hang? I think not. No, Banning, I'm going to kill you, and the law won't be able to touch me for it. After all, you are an escaped criminal who broke into my home, intending me harm. I will be well within my rights to defend myself against my attacker."

"Tell me *why!*"

"I did it because your father could have ruined me. You see, when I found that creek, I learned it originated on Cheyenne land. The rights to that water belong to them. I promised to pay them for its use, but I never did. Why waste money on savages? Your father discovered my secret. He also learned I was inflating the price of the water and pocketing the difference. If I'd let him live, he would have exposed me."

Foy moved still closer. He was not really aware of his movement because he was completely absorbed in this revelation. "How? How did you do it? I know you hit him in the back of the head with something. What did you use?" Foy was totally engaged in this now.

"That was easy. I used a branding iron. It was over in an instant." He grinned. "And so was he."

"You son of a bitch—"

In that instant, Renquist ducked and spun around. His arm came up first, knocking the rifle out of the way. He charged at Foy, aiming at his chest.

Unprepared to resist, Foy folded under Renquist's weight. He felt the breath go out of him and the crushing weight of Renquist's body on his as he landed heavily on his back. His hand released the gun. He struggled to pull free, but Renquist already had command of the situation, jamming an elbow into Foy's ribs as he crawled to cover Foy's body and reach a position from which he could strike. They scrambled for control. Foy felt the pain of the impact and the continuing assault. Left wide open, he was pinned in place. He squirmed to break free as Renquist delivered a blow to his jaw that, while weak, further disabled him, sending streaks of pain through his head.

Realizing he was at a disadvantage, Foy sought to get out from under Renquist's body. In desperation, he managed to free one leg. Pulling it up toward his hip, he forced his foot under Renquist's stomach. With every ounce of strength he had left, Foy pushed and straightened his leg, forcing Renquist away from him.

Momentum carried Renquist up and back. He landed on unsteady feet, but continued to move until he hit the window behind him. The glass shattered as he plummeted through it and he landed heavily on the porch.

BESIDE THE PORCH, SHAWNEE SAW Renquist burst through the window and land hard on the porch floor. Although disoriented, he scrambled to stand up, cutting his hands on the glass shards that had rained down from the broken window. Still, he managed to get up, round the hay bale and step off the porch while lifting the revolver from his holster.

Shawnee moved forward across the porch. "Hey!"

Renquist stopped cold, hesitated for a split second, then he spun around and fired. His shot missed. Shawnee pulled his trigger almost at the same instant. The bullet slammed into Renquist's shoulder, throwing him heavily on his back. His gun landed on the ground beside him, within reach. He tried to roll his body to get to it with his free hand.

Shawnee took a few long steps forward and kicked the weapon away. Renquist collapsed to a supine position. Shawnee stood over him, his gun aimed directly at Renquist's heart.

Behind him, Shawnee heard Foy's voice. "He's mine."

Shawnee's eyes remained locked on the wounded man. "He ain't going nowhere."

Foy stepped off the porch and approached. He pointed the rifle at Renquist and cocked the piece. "For what he did, he's going straight to his maker, straight to hell."

Shawnee stood there for a moment, pondering. "We got him dead to rights, brother. We should ought to let the law handle him."

Foy shook his head. "No. With the connections he's got, he'll weasel out of it. He's got to pay up now."

"Can't let you do that." Shawnee swung his gaze to Foy. "Take it from me, there ain't no coming back from something like that. He ain't worth throwing your life away."

Foy stood his ground. His finger wrapped around the trigger. "I'm killing a murderer. He deserves no better."

"But *you* do. Think about it, boy. You're headed to become a doc, somebody that saves folks' lives. You want to chuck all that over this miserable piece of shit?" Shawnee took an extreme course to head this off. He turned his gun on Foy. "I'll shoot you my own self if it'll wake you up."

Foy turned his head toward Shawnee, an astonished look on his face. "You'd do that?"

"Damn right I will, if'n it'll save you from the life I lead. You got to see it, Foy, the wrong of it. You got to."

The boy appeared to stop and think. They stood there for a long moment, Foy's rifle on Renquist, Shawnee's revolver on Foy. Then, slowly, Foy lowered the rifle's hammer on the live round in the chamber and let the gun sink to his side, muzzle down.

Renquist's sigh of relief was more than noticeable.

Foy winced. "I hope you're right."

"I know I be." Shawnee holstered his gun. "Reckon it's about time I pull up stakes 'fore Driskill decides to come calling."

"After all you did to help with this, I can't see him turning on you."

"He's a lawman. That's what they do—arrest criminals. And, when you come right down to it, that's what I be, a wanted criminal. Believe me, I know when it's time to move on."

"Listen, Shawnee, I can't thank you enough for what you did, and I'll sure miss you."

"Yup. Me, too. You take care of yourself, kid, you hear?"

Shawnee extended his hand. Foy shook it as he smiled and nodded. Shawnee shot a final, hateful glare at Renquist who lay nursing his wound. Then he turned away and started walking toward where the horses were tied. After a few steps, he turned to face Foy.

"Look, when you see Meelee, tell her...." Shawnee shook his head. "Nah, never mind. Reckon she knows."

He turned away and kept walking. It was a slow walk. He was tired, drained. Not only physically, but his mind was weary, as well.

As he approached Gray, though fatigued, his mind raced. This was a solitary life that had been forced on him and he knew he had no choice but to live it out the way it unfolded. There was too much against him to expect anything different. Still, he had signed on to help Foy and he took comfort in the fact that he had done that. Foy would not become an outlaw. Meelee had been a bright spot in this incident. He knew he would never forget her, but he also knew a life with her would never be. That was the sad part. His life would go on until it ended, Lord only knew how. Until then, he could control how he lived his life. Doing things like helping Foy was all that was left for him.

All in all, he reckoned, that wasn't half bad.

Slowly, he mounted and pulled Gray around, heading west.

20

FROM THE CORNER OF HIS eye, Foy saw movement as the man Shawnee had slugged regained consciousness and attempted to get up. Foy hurried to him and helped him to his feet. "You don't work for Renquist anymore. If you've got the sense you were born with, you'll get out of here while you still can."

Nursing the knot on his head, the man mumbled something that Foy took to be agreement. Still unsteady, the man turned toward the barn and stumbled away. Foy returned to Renquist to find him trying in vain to get up.

"You're only making that wound worse. Lay still. I'll patch you up."

"Why would you do that?" Renquist winced in pain. "Why would you help me?"

Foy crouched beside him. "It's what I do. Shawnee showed me that. I'm not like you. I guess I'm not a killer, after all."

FOY LED THE HORSE, WITH Renquist aboard, slowly into Bodeen's main street. It was close to noon. Renquist's wound had been cleaned and bandaged and his arm was cradled in a sling made from a shirt, a dead man's shirt. Foy stopped the horses at the hitch rail near the jail. After dismounting, he helped Renquist down and ushered him to the door of the building.

The door opened just as they reached it. Driskill stepped into the doorway. "Good timing, Banning. I just now finished taking the coroner's statement. Come on in."

Foy directed Renquist inside the jail, allowing Renquist to see Dr. Janes seated beside the desk and Meelee standing behind him.

"That your doing?" Driskill indicated Renquist's wound.

"No. That was Shawnee."

"Uh-huh. And where's he at, anyhow?"

"He decided it was time to leave."

"Just as well. I would have hated to arrest him again. Speaking of which—" Driskill turned his attention to Renquist. "Just to make it official, Renquist, you're under arrest for the murders of Jeremy Banning and Brent Talkot."

"Don't be ridiculous. You have no proof of any of that."

"I don't reckon that'll be a problem. Not according to Doctor Janes, anyway. The way he tells it, you done both of them in and paid him to cover 'em up. He was real eager to unload the whole story after your hired killer mucked up trying to put him down. I got it all down in writing. All signed and sealed."

Renquist said no more. He simply glared at Janes, who cowered in his chair and looked away.

Driskill turned again to Foy and handed him the cell key.

"I'll give you the privilege of locking him up. I'll be taking the doctor over to the hotel and locking *him* in a room. Putting him in the same cell with this one wouldn't work out too healthy for the good doctor."

Foy smirked. "Happy to."

He moved Renquist to the cell and locked him in. When he finished, Driskill took Janes by the arm and led him out of the office.

"Are you all right?" Meelee indicated the cuts on Foy's face.

"I'm fine."

"And Shawnee?"

"He's all right, but he thought it best for him to leave. There would have been trouble if Driskill tried to arrest him again."

"I know." She paused. "I just wish I... could have said goodbye."

"I think this is the way he wanted it."

Meelee nodded. A tear welled in her eye.

She turned away.

FOY SPENT THE NIGHT IN his hotel room, trying in vain to rest from the rigors of the previous day. He wrestled with yet unanswered questions regarding the disposition of the Sorrel Creek Dam. What was he, as Jeremy Banning's legal heir, permitted to do? Could he legally destroy the dam and see that the Cheyenne were repaid for Renquist's encroachment on their land? What were Renquist's retained rights in this affair? Indeed, what were his own rights and responsibilities? The answers escaped him, causing countless sleepless hours. He resolved to spend as much time as necessary tracking down these resolutions.

After a quick breakfast, he showed up at the bank as it opened for business and presented himself to the bank president. "My name is Foy Banning. I'm Jeremy Banning's son and heir. I need to see the records and legal documents regarding the partnership in the Sorrel Creek Dam."

Perusal of those papers consumed most of the day and provided the answers to many questions. For those still remaining, he was directed to the town council's records. There the facts became clear, allowing him to begin formulating a plan.

As dusk began transitioning into night, Foy rode out to Meelee's house. He dismounted and knocked lightly on the door. Meelee opened it. She wore an apron over her gingham dress. She greeted him with a smile. "Good evening, Foy. You're looking better today. I hope you got some rest."

"Evening, Meelee. Actually, I didn't. But I did get some answers. Do you have a moment?"

"Of course, please come in."

She stepped aside to admit him and then closed the door. He could smell food cooking in the kitchen and assumed it was her evening meal.

"Dinner is almost ready," she said. "Will you stay?"

"No, thank you. I have some work to do tonight. I went through the records of the dam and I wanted to tell you what I've learned. Seems the partnership agreement between my father and Renquist is still in force. It was never dissolved. Since I'm Papa's heir, that makes me Renquist's partner now. That means I have an equal say in the disposition of the dam. And, since he has no heir listed, once he's convicted and hanged, I'll have complete control." He allowed his contentment with the developments to come through in his expression and his voice. "I'm going to verify all of this with Uncle Charles's attorney, but I think this will allow me to have the dam dismantled. That should put the Sorrel Creek back on its original course. The ranchers will have water again and they won't have to pay for it. I also found enough money in the account to make an offer of payment to the Cheyenne. That should make things right with them."

Meelee came close to him and put her hand on his arm. "That's wonderful. I'm so glad this worked out the way it has. And I'm so proud of you and what you've become. I know Jeremy is smiling from above."

He smiled broadly. "That's the best compliment I could ever get. I want to thank you for all your help in this. I could never have done it alone. In fact, if you hadn't brought it up, I wouldn't have even known about it."

"It needed to be done. I kept quiet for far too long. I feel so much better now that it's over."

"So do I. Well, I just wanted you to know what I found out. I'm going back to Bodeen now. I need to get my thoughts together and then write that letter to the lawyer. And, tomorrow, I can go to Denver to post it. I'm hoping the answer will come by the time the trial ends so I can take care of this properly. I need to be in California before classes start in September."

"I understand, but why not stay to dinner?"

Foy reached his hand to her cheek tenderly. "I can't. I need to do this right away, but I'll come by when I get back from Denver. We'll have more time then." He turned for the door. "Goodnight, Meelee."

"Goodnight."

He went to the door and let himself out.

Disappointed with Foy's short visit, but satisfied with his prediction of future events, Meelee returned to the kitchen to finish her cooking.

"Evening, Meelee."

Shawnee's voice, while soft in tone, startled her. She looked across the kitchen. Shawnee stood in front of the open window. Apparently, that was his entry point. "Foy told me you left."

He smiled and removed his hat.

"Well, yeah, I did. Had full intent to keep on riding, but I had to see you again. Just once more."

"I'm glad you came back."

Smiling, she took a step toward him. He did the same. At that instant, they both started to speak. Each stopped to defer to the other, causing neither to continue. They chuckled over that.

Meelee paused. "I wanted to at least say goodbye."

"I wanted that, too. Look, I know this is unsettling. I'm real sorry things're like they are. I shoulda just kept on riding, I know that, but when I thought of you and how I left it, I just... I *had* to come back. Look, I'm sorry. I know this ain't doing no good." He turned toward the window. "I'm just going to go."

She took another step, putting her less than a foot from him. There was an ache inside her, urging her to reach out to him, to draw him to her, to embrace him. Tears welled up in her eyes as she realized none of these things would change the fact that this probably was the last time she would ever see him. Wanting to prolong their time together for as long as possible, her mind concocted a delaying action.

"No. Wait. I don't even know your name, your real name, I mean."

Emotion caught in her throat. Her voice was scratchy. Still, her question accomplished its purpose, it delayed Shawnee's exit.

He turned back. "What?"

"Your name. You weren't born being called Shawnee, were you?"

"Reckon not." He chuckled. "No, it's Lon. Lon Pearce."

"How did you come by Shawnee?"

"It's where I come from—Shawneetown, back in Kansas. Back then, Lon Pearce wound up on a wanted poster, so Shawnee kind of stuck, I reckon."

"It's a strong name, I think. Your real name, I mean...."

"I should go."

She took another step closer, her body almost in contact with his.

Her hand went to his forearm. She stopped thinking and allowed her emotions to take over. "Lon."

Before he could speak, she kissed him. It was a soft kiss, nothing more than a touching of her lips to his. That was the way it began, but she lingered there. When he did not pull away, she became more intense. Then he kissed her back. His arm wrapped around her waist and pressed her to him. Her arms raised, almost involuntarily, and her hands caressed the back of his neck. She ignored the scratchiness of his stubble on her lips as she pulled his head closer to her. They were locked in place for several seconds.

The kiss ended and they embraced. She made an unintelligible sound at the contact of their bodies and she strove to press closer.

He whispered in her ear, "Meelee, I—"

"I know. I know you have to go. I know this can never be. But stay a little while, won't you? Give me that at least, please."

"I can't. You know I can't. Every minute I'm here puts you in that much more danger. That deputy walks through that door, he'll arrest you along with me."

She sniffed back a tear. "I don't care." She hung onto him tightly.

"Oh, Meelee, you got to care. You got your whole life ahead of you. Me, I'll be lucky to make it through the year."

She leaned back so he could see her face. "Don't say that. We can go away. Mexico, maybe—or Canada. Anywhere." She was crying now, desperate to keep him with her.

"I can't do that to you. I won't make you an outlaw, make you live a life that ain't right for you. I love you too much to do that to you."

"I love you, too. I want to be with you." She fought to hold on but he pulled back from the embrace and looked her in the eye.

"You don't know what it's like, always looking over your shoulder, wondering if the law's waiting for you 'round the next bend. You sleep, but you don't sleep. The only friends you got is a horse and a gun. No, that ain't for you."

"Even if I want it?"

"Because you want it is why I can't let it be. I shouldn't a came back. I know that." He turned away to face the window. "I got to go... now."

"Lon, please."

"You think on it, you'll see I'm right." His voice cracked a little. He spoke without looking at her. "I'll keep you with me always. I'll never forget you."

He took the last step to the window and climbed out quickly. She moved to the window to see him, but darkness prevented it. The rustle of brush under his boots and the sound of a horse riding away were all that remained, all she could hear.

Then he was gone.

"I love you , Lon," she said into the night. "I always will."

DESPITE BEING A BORN-AND-bred New Yorker who lived most of his life in New Jersey, Bob Giel was a cowboy at heart and lived by the cowboy code. When most of the world today laughs at the quaint and seemingly antiquated concept of honor, he embodied it. Always faithful. Always loyal. Always giving his best effort. Always honest. And perhaps most importantly, keeping his word no matter what. Those values weren't just an act or an affectation, but something he worked at and recommitted to every day. Sadly, Bob passed away in early 2023, but his work and his ethos will continue to live on in his writing.

BOB GIEL

AUTHOR OF A CROW TO PLUCK

SHAWNEE

THE ADVENTURE BEGINS

NOW AVAILABLE AT ALL YOUR FAVORITE BOOKSELLERS